THE DEVIL
DEFEATED

❧

From the library of

Name_____

Address_____

_____

_____

THE ROMANTIC NOVELS OF

BARBARA CARTLAND

❧

THE DEVIL DEFEATED

Barbara Cartland

Eaglemoss Publications Limited
7 Cromwell Road
London SW7 2HR

First published 1985

Set in Sabon
Made and printed in Great Britain by
Richard Clay (The Chaucer Press) Ltd,
Bungay, Suffolk

ISBN 0 947837 59 0

AUTHOR'S NOTE

In the second half of the 19th Century in France there was an upswerve of Black Magic.

This was practised mostly by the intelligentsia who formed Satanical cults that celebrated the Black Mass, attempted to conjure up spirits, studied the prolongation of life and other occult sciences.

In Britain it was mostly confined to the countryside where witches and witchcraft had flourished since the beginning of time. In Eastern England the fear of witchcraft was always intense and the Devil was reputed to be very active in Essex where wizards were plentiful.

Nothing, however, superseded the fantastic orgies of Hell Fire Caves where in the 18th Century Sir Francis Dashwood celebrated Black Mass more grandly than anyone had done before or since. The Caves are still open to the public at High Wycombe in Buckinghamshire.

THE DEVIL DEFEATED

Dorina Stanfield, the elder daughter of the Vicar of the small village of Little Sodbury on the Estate of the Earl of Yardcombe, is worried by the reports of the parties given by the new Earl.

The Earl inherited unexpectedly after his cousins had been killed at Waterloo and when he arrives at Yarde House for the week-end with a number of raffish friends and actresses, she takes every precaution to prevent him from coming into contact with her younger sister who is very beautiful.

However, when one of the Earl's guests assaults one of the village girls who is working up at the Big House, she is brave enough to confront the Earl and take him to task for such outrageous behaviour.

The Earl is astonished, but at the same time he is honest enough to realise that what she is saying is just and when he looks into the behaviour of his servants who were engaged while he was away in the Army of Occupation, he finds that they are corrupt and also dishonest.

Having dismissed them he is therefore obliged to seek Dorina's help to replenish his household and learns incredulously that his heir-apparent, his cousin, is actually intent on killing him so that he can inherit.

How the wicked cousin Jarvis Yarde's plans are foiled by Dorina, but not before he has tried among other things black magic, is told in this strange and fascinating 376th book by Barbara Cartland.

CHAPTER ONE
1818

"Who do you think I have just seen?"

Rosabelle burst into the Dining-Room as she spoke, and her sister Dorina looked up from the end of the table where she was spooning a pleasantly smelling stew onto a plate and said sharply:

"You are late, Rosabelle."

"I know," she replied, "and I am sorry, but I have seen the Earl!"

"Where did you see him?" Peter asked with his mouth full.

"In the Park," Rosabelle replied.

Dorina walked round the table to put the plate of stew she had just served in front of her sister and said crossly:

"I have told you before, Rosabelle – and you have to listen to me – you must not go into the Park now that the new Earl is home, unless he invites you to do so!"

"We have always been allowed to go in the Park," Rosabelle replied. "Why should he stop us?"

"Because he owns it, silly!" Peter answered.

Peter was eleven and at the age when he thought all girls were silly anyway, and he added as if his sister did not understand:

"He could have you up for trespassing if he wanted to, so Dorina is right – we should keep out of the Park."

Rosabelle pouted and she looked very pretty as she did so.

"I think you are all very disagreeable!" she said. "It was very exciting seeing the Earl. He was riding with three other very handsome gentlemen."

"Did he see you?" Dorina asked.

"I was with Rover in the bushes, and I crouched down so that he would not see me."

"You must promise me not to go in the Park again," Dorina said in a firm voice, "and that includes the woods!"

Rosabelle and Peter gave cries of protest.

"But we must go in the woods, Dorina, we always have! If they are out of bounds as well as the Park, we will only be able to walk along the dusty road which will be terribly boring!"

"I know, I know," Dorina agreed, "but please, do as I say! I am sure if the Earl sees you he will think you are intruding, and that would be a mistake."

"I do not see why," Rosabelle said rebelliously.

She was just fifteen and at the age when she resented being told not to do something. At the same time, like Peter, she loved her elder sister and as a general rule they were both extremely obedient. Since Dorina after her mother's death, had taken over the running of the household, she had in fact, found they were very little trouble.

The door of the Dining-Room opened and her father came in.

The Reverend Prosper Stanfield was an exceedingly good-looking man.

His hair which was just beginning to turn grey was

a little untidy, and there was a vague look in his eyes which meant that he had been enjoying his work in the garden and had no wish to be taken away from it for anything so unnecessary as a meal.

The Vicar had always been intensely interested in gardening and especially in developing rare species of cactus.

But since his wife's death, which had made him so desperately unhappy that Dorina had feared for a time that he might take his life, he had concentrated fiercely on his gardening to help him forget his loneliness.

Now she noted as he sat down at the table that he had remembered to wash his hands and she said gently in a voice that showed how much she loved him:

"Have you had a good morning, Papa? I am sure your plants are doing well in the sunshine."

"They are, indeed!" her father replied. "In fact, I think that last one which you laughed at because it was so small, is at last beginning to grow."

"You must show it to me after luncheon," Dorina said.

She walked round the table to put his plate of stew in front of him and handed him the vegetables.

She noted as she did so that Rosabelle had taken so little cabbage that it was almost invisible on her plate.

Peter however had helped himself to so many potatoes that there were only three left for his father.

Dorina, however, said nothing and having poured out a glass of cider for her father which was a present from a local farmer, went back to her own chair to help herself to what was left of the stew and vegetables.

Although she never complained, it was very difficult to provide food the family enjoyed without overspending the very small allowance her father could give her for the house-keeping.

If it had not been for Nanny's skill in managing to get an occasional duck, chicken or pigeon out of the farmer's wives who came to Church in Sunday, they would have existed on a permanent diet of rabbit and scrag end of beef because it was cheap.

Nanny was a good but plain cook, and everything that came to the table, while nourishing, was not exciting.

However Dorina could not think only about food, for she had too many other worries; the most important being at the moment how they could afford to send Peter to a good School, preferably Eton, where his father and his grandfather had gone before him.

If she was not worrying about Peter, it was about Rosabelle who was growing into a pretty young woman who was becoming exceedingly conscious of her appearance.

She was therefore continually asking for new gowns, bonnets and shoes, all of which, unfortunately, cost money.

Now because she was annoyed with Dorina for rebuking her Rosabelle said to her father:

"What do you think, Papa? I saw the new Earl this morning! He was riding the most magnificent horse, a black stallion, which is quite different from anything that has been in the Yarde stables before."

"The new Earl?" the Vicar repeated as if his thoughts were far away. "He has certainly taken a long time in coming home."

"He has been in France," Dorina said, "with the Army of Occupation, and it is only recently that its numbers are being reduced and so many soldiers are returning."

"Yes, yes, of course," her father replied, "and it is a good thing that Yarde will have somebody to look after it again, and of course, the Estate."

"I hope the Earl will realise what should be done," Dorina said in a slightly repressive tone.

Her father did not answer and Rosabelle said:

"I heard Mrs. Champion telling Nanny they had a riotous house-party up at the Big House this week-end. She said there were ladies glittering like Christmas trees, and the amount the gentlemen drank must have emptied half the cellar!"

"That is only gossip," Dorina exclaimed, "and you should not repeat such things!"

"I am only telling you what Mrs. Champion said to Nanny."

"I do not suppose they knew you were listening!"

"How could I help it," Rosabelle asked, "when Mrs. Champion is so deaf that she always shouts?"

Dorina decided it was undignified to go on arguing.

She thought it was a mistake for Rosabelle to be too interested in what was happening since the Earl's return.

She tried to change the conversation by talking to her father about his garden.

But the children were thrilled that something new was occurring in the quiet village of Little Sodbury, where everything appeared to be the same, month in, month out.

"I would like to see the Earl's horses," Peter was saying, "and I suppose there is no chance of my riding one?"

"You are to stay away from the stables!" Dorina said. "As I told you to do, as soon as the Earl arrived four days ago!"

"They like my going there," Peter protested. "Old Hawkins says I am as good at rubbing down a horse as any of his stable-lads, and you know, Dorina, he has let me ride around the paddock dozens of times."

"That was very different. We knew the old Earl very well and he was very fond of us," Dorina said. "I have explained to you both over and over again, that we cannot take advantage or impose ourselves on the new Earl until we have met him, and until he proves to be as kind as his uncle was."

"Suppose he does not want to be kind to us?" Rosabelle asked. "Then what are we to do?"

"Manage on our own!" Dorina said sharply.

She looked across the table at her father whose thoughts were obviously far away, and after a moment she said:

"I was wondering, Papa, as the Earl did not come to Church on Sunday, whether it would be correct for you to call on him?"

The Vicar looked at her for a moment as if what she had said had hardly penetrated his mind. Then he replied:

"I expect, if His Lordship wants me, he will send for me. In the meantime, I am too busy, my dear, to drive up to Yarde, only to find it to be a wasted journey."

Dorina did not point out to him that it would take him less than ten minutes to drive from the village up to the front door of the Big House.

She had, however, the uncomfortable feeling it might well be a waste of time if in fact the Earl had no wish to see her father and sent him away.

She therefore said quietly:

"I am sure you are right, Papa. Perhaps we shall see him in Church next Sunday."

She thought as she spoke that it was very unlikely.

14

The whole village had been desperately disappointed that after the Earl's arrival at his ancestral home four days ago, there had been no one in the Yarde family pew at any of the Services that took place on Sunday.

The congregations because they were not unnaturally curious, had been larger than they had been for some time, and even Dorina had found herself glancing continually in the direction of the West Door until the Service started.

Now, because of what she had heard since the new Earl's arrival – and gossip flew on wings round the small village – she was quite certain he was not a Church-goer and if they should ever meet him it would be by chance, rather than by his showing any interest.

Carrying the plates and the empty bowl which had contained the stew into the kitchen, she found Nanny dishing up a large sponge pudding and covering it with strawberry jam.

"Mind your father has a big helping," she said as she fetched the warm plates from the oven, "he's not eating enough at the moment to keep a mouse alive."

"He ate all the stew I gave him," Dorina said, "and I think he enjoyed it. It was delicious, Nanny."

"I does me best," Nanny said sharply, "but no one can make bricks without straw, and unless you're all to starve next week, you'll have to ask your father for some more money."

"It is no use, Nanny. He has none," Dorina replied. "I did the accounts with him last night, and he was wondering how he could afford to buy a new cactus that he had heard was growing well in Kew Gardens."

"Well, all I can say," Nanny said tartly, "is for goodness sake, Miss Dorina, persuade the Vicar to grow food, especially vegetables."

15

Dorina laughed, and it was a very pretty sound.

"Mama tried that once, but she failed, Papa really loves his cactus, and I have often thought it is because he has always wanted to travel to visit Africa and Brazil! As he plants and grows his cactuses that is what he is doing in his imagination."

"And that's about all we can afford these days," Nanny said as she handed Dorina the plates and put the pudding gently on top of them.

Then she opened the kitchen door and Dorina carried the food into the Dining-Room.

When she had gone Nanny gave a sigh and sat down on one of the hard chairs by the kitchen-table.

She was over sixty, and after she had been standing for a long time her legs hurt her.

In the winter she often had a touch of rheumatism which hurt her even more.

But she was not thinking of herself or her aches and pains, but of the children she had loved ever since they were born, and how unfair it seemed that they should have to try to exist on so little when, according to reports, money was being thrown about like water up at the Big House.

Everything that happened in Little Sodbury was related to Nanny almost as if she had a right to it.

She had been the first person to be told when the new Earl arrived, and every detail about his guests who came down from London the next day was hurriedly carried to the Vicarage.

It was not surprising that the inhabitants of the village who were all living in houses owned by the Earl of Yardcombe were interested in their new master.

Living on the estate of Yarde, which was one of the great ancestral houses in England, they had all from the oldest pensioner to the youngest child, taken it for granted that the 6th Earl's son William would inherit when his father died.

They had known William from the moment he was born, and to the older people in the village and on the estate it was almost as if he was their own son.

They had watched him through every age and learnt when he had measles and whooping-cough that he suffered rather worse than their own children.

They were delighted when he was old enough to go out hunting with his father, and thrilled when he shot his first rabbit and caught his first fish in the lake.

William was one of themselves and they looked on him with love and admiration, and as he grew older, with a possessive pride.

There was no one who did not suffer agonisingly when William was killed fighting the French on the Peninsula.

Although their affection and interest was quickly turned to his younger brother Charles, when in turn he was killed in an accident in Belgium during the manoeuvring of Wellington's new Army a month before the Battle of Waterloo, they were again shattered.

To Dorina, who had been virtually brought up with both of the young men, it had left a scar that had hardly yet healed.

Because they had been children together, the boys had run in and out of the Vicarage as she was able to run in and out of the Big House. She had felt indeed as if they were her brothers, and when they were gone there was an unfilled gap in her life.

It seemed impossible to realise that William, who was two years older than herself and Charles who was one year younger, would never return, while the title and the Big House would go to a cousin whom she had never seen and about whom they knew nothing.

The old Earl's first cousin had lived abroad a great deal of his life, and his son Oscar, although he was educated in England, had always spent his holidays abroad.

Dorina had learned that he had gone straight from School into the Army, and apparently made a great success of his career, rising rapidly from Captain to Major, and ending the war as a Colonel.

Actually that was all anybody knew about him.

He had never come to Yarde and the old Earl, who had always tried to be a father-figure to all his relatives, had never talked about him to Dorina's knowledge. In fact, it was doubtful if he had ever met him.

"How can God be so cruel, Papa, as to allow both William and Charles to be killed?" she had asked her father. "Who is there left who really cares about us, or the people who have looked to the Earl of Yardcombe to protect and guide them, as the last Earl did?"

Her father had put his hand on her shoulder to show he understood what she was feeling and said:

"Many strange things happen in life, my dearest. While one rebels against them, it often happens that things turn out to be right when we least expect it."

"I cannot see how it can possibly be right for both William and Charles to be killed!" Dorina had said angrily.

"I miss them, as you do," the Vicar agreed, "and as I miss your mother."

There was a pain in his voice which made Dorina know she was being very selfish by speaking of her own unhappiness when she knew that every moment of his life was a torture because he was alone and his wife was no longer with him.

They had been so happy together that it had never mattered if they had so little money, or if the Vicar gave away far too much of what little they did have to the people who begged from him.

The Vicarage itself was shabby and very much in need of paint, but because the family always seemed to be laughing the rooms were filled with sunshine, and people who visited them did not notice that the curtains were faded, the carpets worn, and the furniture needed to be repaired.

Then Mrs. Stanfield had died one cold December night when nothing they could do seemed to make the rooms any warmer.

She had caught a cold while visiting a parishioner who was dying in the village. It had turned to pneumonia and almost before they could realise it, she had left them.

The Vicar was so distraught that Dorina was afraid she would lose her father as well as her mother.

Somehow they had survived, and now when she was secretly hoping that perhaps the new Earl would understand how prices had increased since the war and would raise her father's stipend, the story of the party taking place in the Big House did nothing to reassure her that any improvements were likely.

It seemed incredible that the Earl should not have come down alone, or at least with perhaps one friend, to get to know his household, the people on the Estate, and of course his neighbours.

The first thing they learned on his return to England, was that he had opened the house in London which because the last Earl had been an old man and in ill-health, had been closed for years.

Before then he had sent a new Manager to Yarde to make changes before he could return from France, but to the villagers the changes were horrifying.

Old Burrows the Butler, who had been at Yarde for

over forty years, had been retired, so was Mrs. Meadows, the Housekeeper, and a number of the other members of the household staff were moved out with her.

At first the inhabitants of Little Sodbury could hardly believe what was happening.

They all called on Nanny to discuss it in the kitchen of the Vicarage, and Dorina could hear their voices rising and falling, but always with the same note of condemnation which seemed to echo round the passages and anywhere else she happened to be in the house.

She could understand so well what they were feeling.

Because the people in the village had always thought of themselves as being part of the Yarde family, they would say, just as the servants at the Big House said: "We will be doing this," and "We will be doing that."

The new Manager was a young man who Dorina learned had been in the Army with Oscar Yarde before he came into the title.

She had not met him, but she had seen him walking about the village, inspecting some of the houses, and going into 'The Green Dragon' where it was reported he drank an inordinate amount of brandy and showed no interest in sampling the local ale.

He was a rather cocky-looking man, and she suspected he was not exactly a gentleman, but she tried not to condemn him as the rest of the village had from the moment he arrived.

"I says to him," she heard one of the servants from the Big House say: "'That's how it's always been done, Sir' and he says to me: 'Well, the sooner there are changes here the better'."

Changes, changes – after that it was all anybody

could talk about, and old Burrows, who had always seemed to her to look like a benevolent Bishop, moved into a dilapidated cottage which had been offered to him on his retirement.

Now he looked only a sad, elderly little man who had somehow lost what had always been very precious to him, his pride.

"That man has no right to be in His Lordship's place!" Nanny said angrily after she had heard of several more changes that had been made up at the Big House. "If I ever gets the chance, I'll give him a piece of my mind!"

Dorina thought with a faint sense of amusement that was what a lot of other people also would like to do, and she herself felt the same.

"How can he allow such things to happen without first coming here to see for himself?" she asked.

Then as she despaired of the new Earl ever appearing, she woke up one morning to be told that he had arrived unexpectedly, late the night before, and was arranging for a large party to join him for the week-end.

"It is not the way he should have taken over his Kingdom," she said to herself.

That, she thought, was exactly what Yarde was: a Kingdom for any man who understood how fortunate he was to have inherited a crown that had been lost by two young men who had died for their country.

"I think I hate him!" Dorina had said when Sunday had passed without there being anybody in the Yarde family pew at Church.

And stories were already buzzing around the village as to what was happening 'up at the Big House'.

She tried not to listen, but it was impossible not to be interested in the ladies whose faces, according to one of the housemaids, were powdered and painted as if they were appearing in a Play House.

There were stories too of gentlemen whose behaviour was whispered only to Nanny, so that she was not quite certain what they had done but, whatever it was, it was exceedingly reprehensible.

As Dorina finished washing up the dishes they had used for luncheon Nanny said:

"I'm going down to the village to see if I can find anything for supper. There's not a thing in the house, but I doubt if Mr. Banks will let us have much more credit!"

Mr. Banks was the Butcher, and Dorina was continually ashamed of how long he often had to wait to be paid the Vicarage account, even if it was not a very large one.

"I will talk to Papa tonight," she said to Nanny, "but I doubt if he can spare me a penny until next month."

"By that time we'll all be in our graves!" Nanny said sharply. "If you asks me someone should point out to the new Earl that instead of wasting his money on wine and women who are no better than they should be, he ought to be doing something for those who are his responsibility and no one else's!"

That was what Dorina felt too, but there was no point in saying so.

Putting on her black bonnet and a shawl over her shoulders, Nanny set off with her string-bag in her hand.

Dorina, having watched her go, thought she might go into the garden and join her father.

She had the feeling, however, that he did not really want to be disturbed and she wondered instead if she might go for a walk.

Then she remembered that as she had forbidden Rosabelle and Peter to go into the Park or in the woods, she must observe the same ban.

It seemed incredible that the woods, which had meant so much to her ever since she was a small child, should now be out of bounds.

She knew that Rosabelle had been right when she said it was boring to have only the dusty lanes to walk along, instead of moving over the mossy paths beneath the high trees.

To Dorina the woods had an enchantment which never failed to soothe away any unhappiness she might be feeling.

They had for her, a magic that it was impossible to put into words, but it was there every time she moved amongst the trees and heard the birds fluttering in the boughs above her.

She felt she had stepped from the humdrum existence of everyday life into a world where dreams came true, and for her the fairies she had believed in as a child were, she was half-convinced, still real.

There were goblins who had been far more real than those she read about in books and even now, when she was grown up and, she told herself, sensible, she still found herself thinking there must be dragons in the great fir woods which lay to the North.

"If I cannot go into the woods," she asked herself, "then where can I go?"

She felt a surge of anger against the new Earl that was a culmination of everything that had gone wrong ever since William had been killed.

Deep in thought, she was suddenly aware of a knock on the back door.

Knowing Nanny was still out and there was no one else to answer it except herself, she hurried down the

23

passage into the kitchen and opening the door found outside one of the women from the village.

"Good afternoon, Mrs. Bell!" she said. "I am afraid, if you have come to see Nanny, you have just missed her."

"It's you, Miss Dorina, I really want to see," Mrs. Bell replied in a rather hesitating voice.

Dorina smiled.

"Well, I am here. Come in!"

Mrs. Bell walked in through the open door, and because Dorina sensed she had something important to say she took her not into the kitchen but into a small room where she habitually sat when she wanted to be on her own.

Mrs. Bell was obviously impressed and Dorina said:

"Come and sit down, Mrs. Bell, and tell me what is worrying you. I hope there is nothing wrong with Mary and that she is happy working at the Big House."

"It's about Mary I've come to speak to you," Mrs. Bell said. "I suppose really I should see the Vicar, but although I respect your father and I know he's a good man, almost too good for this life, it's just that I feel a little embarrassed, so to speak, and I finds it easier talking to you."

Wondering what all this could be about, Dorina said:

"Of course you can tell me anything you want to, Mrs. Bell, just as I know that if my mother were alive you would have talked to her. So what is wrong?"

Mrs. Bell drew in her breath and told her.

. . . .

Having said goodbye to several of his guests who had arranged to return to London after an early luncheon, the Earl walked into the Library.

He stood for a moment looking at the thousands of

24

books which filled the shelves and constituted one of the most important Libraries in the whole country.

He was thinking that, since he had discovered the majority of them were uncatalogued, he supposed, when he had time to put his mind to it, that he would appoint a Curator.

An inventory could then be made of everything in the house and the books could be properly catalogued.

He walked to the window to look out over the Park where the spotted deer could be seen sheltering in the shadows of the trees from the heat of the afternoon sun.

He thought, as he had from the moment he had arrived, that Yarde was even more impressive than he had ever dreamt it would be.

He could still hardly believe that he was the owner of such magnificence.

It was the same feeling he had had ever since he had learned nearly eighteen months ago that Charles Yarde had been killed and he was therefore the direct heir to the Earl who he had learnt, was dying.

It seemed incredible, completely and absolutely incredible, that he, who had had no prospects except those of rising steadily in the Army, in which he had already achieved a remarkable success, should now through the misfortunes of war have inherited an old and revered title, a house and an estate that he had always heard his father speak of both with awe and respect.

Although he would have liked to visit Yarde it had never been suggested that he should do so, and he had felt no strong interest in it.

Although he had been at Eton like his cousins, they were younger than he was and he could only remember being there with William for less than one year.

He had left Eton to go straight into his father's Regiment, fired with an ambition to distinguish himself and knowing that war gave him an opportunity of doing so which he might never have had in peace-time.

He had enjoyed his life in the Army and, if he was honest, he had enormously enjoyed holding a very important position in the Army of Occupation.

This had been due partly to his outstanding record as a soldier, but equally to the fact that shortly after the Duke of Wellington had established him in France, the old Earl of Yardcombe had died.

To suddenly find himself of great social significance was something Oscar Yarde had never expected or even imagined might ever happen to him.

He soon learnt that his position in life was now very different from what it had been for him as a clever, handsome and very attractive soldier.

At first he was overwhelmed by the attention that was paid to him, not only by the diplomats and politicians, but also by the ladies of the Social World who had never noticed him before.

Because the Duke was living in Paris and his staff with him, as soon as it was safe to do so a large number of attractive women arrived from England.

They all had good excuses for being there – they were either the wives, sisters or *fiancées* of Staff Officers, or had some connection with the British Ambassador which made it imperative for them to assist him in what was at the moment the most important diplomatic post in Europe.

Whatever their reasons for being in Paris, their beauty was alluring and the Earl of Yardcombe found it impossible to escape their blandishments. He would indeed have been inhuman if he had not accepted what was now so readily offered to him.

He was not particularly conceited, but he would have been very stupid if he had not realised that because he was so good-looking and certainly he looked the part in his uniform, women had always gravitated towards him as if to a magnet.

He had therefore found himself involved in numerous love-affairs whenever he was not actually fighting the enemy.

Now when there was plenty of time to enjoy himself as well as work quite hard, for Wellington kept his officers at it, the new Earl found he had moved up many rungs to the top of the social-ladder.

Ladies whom he would never have thought of approaching in the past now sought him out and made it clear what they wanted from him.

There were also in Paris, and this was something in which the French excelled, the most fascinating and alluring Courtesans that any man could wish to find.

That they were expensive went without saying, but it would have been impossible for any man to live in Paris for long without savouring a unique experience which could not be found in any other Capital.

By the time the Army of Occupation on the insistence of the French was being run down and diminished in number, so that quite a number of the Senior Officers could go home, the Earl of Yardcombe's education in the art of l'Amour had opened new horizons and he had become as proficient a lover as he was a soldier.

He had gone back to England finding himself, almost for the first time since he had inherited, really curious about his new possessions and determined to learn everything he could about them as quickly as possible.

He did not feel he had wasted his time in Paris, for he knew it would have been extremely inconvenient not only for himself but for the Duke of Wellington if he had insisted on returning earlier.

He knew now that he had to make up for lost time, and he went first to London to open Yarde House which he had been told was ready to receive him, even though his predecessor had not stayed there for many years before he died.

Yarde House in Berkeley Square was most impressive, and he had no sooner arrived than he was greeted effusively by a cousin he had not even known existed.

He introduced himself as Jarvis Yarde and proceeded to make himself indispensible in a way that the Earl had to admit was extremely convenient.

It was Jarvis who knew who was the best Tailor patronised by the Regent and approved of by all the members of White's, the best Club in London, to which the Earl was promptly introduced and elected as a member.

It was Jarvis also who took him to Wattiers and Carlton House where, to his surprise, the Prince Regent greeted him with open arms and insisted that for the next few days he should be in attendance upon him.

Finally, although not least, Jarvis took him to the most fashionable Houses of Pleasure in St. James's, which although he was too tactful to say so, were not in his opinion anything like as good as those in Paris.

There was so much to do in London, so many people to meet, and suddenly without his conscious intention he found himself involved in a passionate love-affair with Lady Maureen Wilson.

He had met Lady Maureen briefly in Paris and, since her husband was still conveniently engaged in his duties there, she was free to help him enjoy the pleasures of London.

That, the Earl found, meant that he enjoyed her, and Cousin Jarvis waited in the wings until he could command his full attention once again.

It was over three weeks before the Earl said firmly that he intended to go to the country and inspect Yarde.

He intended, and he pointed this out quite carefully, to go down alone, inspect the house and the estate and of course get to know his employees and any neighbours who wished to make his acquaintance.

But Jarvis had other ideas.

"Of course you must go to Yarde," he said.

Then almost before the Earl was aware of what was happening he found he was giving a party for a number of people whose hospitality he had accepted in London, and Lady Maureen was invited as his special guest.

Soon all the State Rooms were ringing with their laughter.

He found himself sitting at the top of the table in the huge Banqueting Hall where his ancestors had sat before him, and whose portraits stared down at him, he hoped approvingly.

The candles in the gold chandeliers glittered, as did the jewels on the heads and round the necks of his lady guests, while their low décolletage, he could not help thinking, would in the past have made him blush.

It was a rowdy, riotous party and he could not help enjoying himself with Lady Maureen, but it gave him no time to do the things he had intended.

Now that most of them had either left or were soon leaving, he told himself severely that he must get down to work.

'I am sure there is a great deal to be done,' he thought with a feeling that was one of excitement.

Here was something new, here was a job as complicated and difficult as if he was going into battle in which success or failure depended entirely upon himself.

He heard the Library door open and turned from the window expecting it to be one of his remaining guests, but the Butler announced:

"Miss Dorina Stanfield, M'Lord!"

A girl came into the room and one glance at her told the Earl that she was very young, very lovely, and extremely badly dressed.

As she walked slowly towards him he became aware with a feeling of surprise that she was looking straight at him and in her large grey eyes was an expression not only of what was unmistakable anger, but also of positive dislike.

CHAPTER TWO

The Earl walked towards Dorina and held out his hand.

"How do you do, Miss Stanfield."

To his surprise she ignored his hand, but dropped him a small curtsy before she said:

"I have called to see you, My Lord, on a very *important* matter."

The way she accentuated the word 'important' made the Earl raise his eye-brows, but he merely said:

"Will you sit down and tell me what this is about?"

For a moment he thought she was going to refuse. Then she walked to an upright chair which seemed somewhat austere amongst the more comfortable ones and sat down on the edge of it.

Her back was straight, her hands in her lap, and, when she looked at him, her eyes were filled with an expression that he knew he had never seen on any woman's face before.

There was a short pause until, as if she was feeling for words, Dorina began:

"I am sure you are not aware, My Lord, that amongst the women your new Housekeeper has engaged, is a young girl called Mary Bell?"

She stressed the word 'new' and the Earl interrupted her to say:

"My *new* Housekeeper? Is there any particular reason, Miss Stanfield, why I should not have one?"

"It is up to you, My Lord," Dorina replied, "to employ whomsoever you choose, but I can hardly believe that what I have just learned from Mary's mother is something which could have happened at Yarde!"

"What has happened?" the Earl asked bluntly.

"Mary Bell is only just sixteen," Dorina said. "She came back to see her mother this morning in a deeply distressed state because last night one of the gentlemen in your party attempted to assault her!"

The way Dorina spoke was an accusation in itself, and as the Earl did not speak she went on:

"Mary ran to the Housekeeper for help, only to be informed that in future she would either do what Your Lordship's friends required of her, or she would be dismissed without a reference and the Housekeeper would see that her family was turned out of their cottage!"

Dorina had managed to speak clearly and slowly. Then, as if her feelings overcame her, she rose to her feet to say furiously:

"How could this sort of thing happen at Yarde of all places, where we have always been so happy and where all the people employed by your uncle felt they were one of the family?"

Now her words seemed to tumble over themselves and she spoke impetuously with an anger that seemed to vibrate through her.

"I suppose," the Earl said, "that you are quite sure of your facts and that what has been reported is not some hysterical fancy of a young girl?"

Dorina drew in her breath.

32

"I might have anticipated, My Lord, that that would be your reaction!"

Now she was even more angry than she had been before.

"Your new Manager has dismissed all the old servants who, as I have already said, felt they were part of the family and were so proud of Yarde that they would never have allowed anything wrong or wicked to happen . . there."

The Earl would have spoken but Dorina continued:

"Instead he has filled their places with servants who would not be tolerated in any decent person's household, let alone your uncle's if he were alive."

"I can hardly believe this is true!" the Earl managed to expostulate.

"If you think I would lie about what is going on, then all I can say is that I am ashamed, deeply humiliated and ashamed, that you should have taken the place of a man who was revered and respected by everybody with whom he came in contact, and . . loved by . . those who . . served him."

She paused not only for breath, but because her voice broke and there were tears in her eyes which she wiped away impatiently.

The Earl rose slowly to his feet. Then he said:

"I think, Miss Stanfield, that we should start again from the beginning. You must first explain to me why you are concerned with what goes on in this house, and also help me to make sure that none of the accusations you have made are exaggerated or untrue."

He spoke in a quiet, conciliatory manner, at the same time with a note of authority which made Dorina feel she had been over-dramatic.

But she was still furiously angry and afraid that the

33

Earl was going to dismiss everything she had said not only as untrue, but also as unimportant.

With what was almost a superhuman effort, knowing that though she wanted to leave him it was important that she should stay, she forced herself to sit down again on the chair.

As she did so the Earl also sat.

As if he had now taken charge, he said still in that quiet voice that somehow took the heat out of the atmosphere between them:

"You were announced as Miss Dorina Stanfield. Do you live in the village?"

"My father, My Lord, is the Vicar."

"Now I understand," the Earl said. "So in everything that occurs which the villagers find distressing they turn to your father for help. But why on this occasion should they have come to you?"

"Mrs. Bell is a respectable, decent woman," Dorina said stiffly, "and she would have been embarrassed to speak to my father of . . such things."

"So she preferred to tell what happened to you, who if you will excuse my saying so, are a very young girl and obviously inexperienced in such matters."

"If you mean by 'inexperienced' that we are not used to such behaviour in Little Sodbury, My Lord, then that is true," Dorina said quickly, "and Mrs. Bell had only me to come to, since my mother is no longer alive. We have always been protected by Yarde and your uncle the Earl set us an example of everything that was fine and noble, and the village tried to live up to him."

Dorina spoke simply in a way that the Earl could not help thinking was very impressive.

Then she went on:

"We also had the example of your uncle's sons,

34

William and Charles, who were loved, respected and emulated by every young man in the village."

She gave the Earl an unmistakable look of hostility before she added:

"I cannot imagine that any of the gentlemen who visited Yarde in the past would have behaved in the same way that your guest did last night, nor that any senior servant could have behaved as your new House-keeper did!"

The Earl was silent for a moment. Then he said:

"I can understand, Miss Stanfield, that what you have heard has shocked you, and I can only deeply regret that any guest of mine, if this is true, should have behaved in such a manner to one of my servants."

"Of course it is true!" Dorina said. "Mary is a very truthful girl and, as anyone in the village will tell you, she is reserved and has always kept herself very much to herself. If you are thinking that perhaps she encouraged the advances of the gentleman in question, I can assure you she was genuinely appalled by what he suggested, and he terrified her, because here in the country we never expected to encounter such .. wickedness."

Before she could say any more the Earl said dryly:

"Then I can only say, Miss Stanfield, that you have been very fortunate!"

He was thinking as he spoke of the behaviour he had seen commonly in France and which he knew was echoed in London amongst the Gentlemen of Fashion who pursued any woman, whatever her status in life, if she attracted them.

The Earl was indeed extremely annoyed that anybody staying in his house should have outraged the sensibilities of a young servant.

35

He wanted, however, before he condemned the gentleman in question, whoever he might be, to be absolutely sure that, as he had said to Dorina, this story was not just the hysterical imagination of a young girl or perhaps one who was making herself out to be more important than she really was.

He was not prepared after his last words, however, for Dorina once again to repeat:

"If you are going to make excuses, My Lord, for what any decent man would say was a disgusting and outrageous incident, then I feel there is nothing more I can say on the matter. I can only ask you, if you have any feelings of justice, not to carry out your Housekeeper's threat and turn the Bells, who have served the Yarde family all their lives, out of their cottage."

"Can you really believe I would do such a thing?" the Earl asked sharply.

He could not help thinking that while it was an experience that had never come his way before to be raged at by a young and very pretty woman, she was really going too far.

"I see no reason why I should not believe it possible," Dorina said. "What has already been done at Yarde by your Manager has horrified everybody who lives on the estate, and my father has been deeply shocked, although he does not feel you would listen to him if he told you so."

"As Vicar of this Parish, I should have thought it was his duty to tell me anything that might be to the detriment of the family name!" the Earl snapped back.

Dorina's eyes widened as she looked at him with what he knew was an expression of astonishment.

"You cannot really think that everyone would not be appalled at the manner in which the old servants were turned out of the house as Burrows was, after forty years of service."

"Who is Burrows?" the Earl asked.

"The Butler. He was noted for training his footmen better than anybody else in the Country, and he kept his silver shining so that you could see your face in it."

Dorina sounded for a moment as if she was talking to herself, then she went on quickly:

"And Mrs. Meadows, the Housekeeper, was turned out with an inadequate pension that will hardly keep her alive, and she was told the only cottage available for her was one in which the roof leaks and half the panes in the windows are cracked."

The Earl was silent, and Dorina said again with a catch in her voice:

"How could you have .. done these things? How could you have been so .. cruel to people who loved William and Charles as if they were their .. own sons and would at any time have .. laid down their lives for .. your uncle?"

Again tears came into her eyes and she turned her back on the Earl and walked away towards the window to stare out into the garden.

He did not speak and after a moment she said in a different tone of voice from the one she had used before:

"This is such a lovely place! Everyone in the village wanted to work here, and as soon as they were old enough to think they began to prepare themselves for coming up to the Big House."

"Are you telling me that attitude has changed?"

"Of course it has changed as a result of your instructions," Dorina answered, "you told Major Richardson, your Manager, to get rid of all the old people, and you raised the rents of the farmers while all the other landlords in the County and doubtless all over England, have lowered theirs because of the crisis in agriculture now that the war is over."

"Is that true?" the Earl asked.

"Once again," Dorina said angrily, "you are doubting my word. If Your Lordship does not believe me, ask Major Richardson to show you the rent-books. Ask anyone you like in the village what has happened to the families who have always served the Yardes from the cradle to the grave, and ask Mary Bell what happened last night!"

Once again the words were tumbling over themselves as Dorina spoke, the Earl could see her slim body silhouetted against the window was trembling with the anger she felt.

What she was saying was completely incredible to him. At the same time, he knew it was something he must investigate immediately.

There was a considerable pause before, as Dorina had apparently no more to say, the Earl remarked:

"You have surprised me, Miss Stanfield, and I must assure you that I had no knowledge whatever of what you tell me has been happening in my absence."

Dorina turned round.

"Are you denying that everything Major Richardson did was on your orders?"

"I sent Major Richardson here from Paris because my duties prevented me from coming myself," the Earl replied. "I learnt that Mr. Andrews who had looked after the estate in my uncle's time had died, and the Solicitors suggested that I appoint a Manager in his place."

"Mr. Andrews was a very conscientious man," Dorina said, "who knew and understood the problems and difficulties of everybody who worked here. Major

Richardson made the changes and gave the orders in your name, and did not even call on my father or anyone else in the vicinity."

The Earl found this hard to believe, but he did not say so. Instead he answered:

"What I am going to suggest, Miss Stanfield, is that you let me find out exactly what has been happening in my absence, then . . ."

Before he could say any more he was interrupted when the door opened and Lady Maureen burst in.

She was dressed ready to return to London in a striking gown of crimson silk with a taffeta pelisse in the same colour which was flung open to reveal that round her neck she was wearing a necklace of rubies and diamonds.

The same stones glittered in the ear-rings which swung beneath her dark hair, half-covered by a bonnet trimmed with ostrich feathers.

She looked flamboyant but at the same time very beautiful, with her face skilfully embellished with powder, rouge and lip-salve as was the fashion.

She swept across the room towards the Earl to say:

"Really, Oscar, how could you be so long when you knew I was waiting for you?"

Then as if she suddenly realised he was not alone she glanced at Dorina and said in an amused voice:

"Are you already taking your Landlord's duties seriously, and can this be one of your pretty milk-maids? My dear, I am quite jealous!"

She was laughing sarcastically as she reached the Earl's side, and putting up her hand to his cheek she added as she did so:

"Poor Oscar! I can see you will soon be involved in all the passionate problems concerning peas, potatoes and pigs."

The Earl removed Lady Maureen's hand from his cheek and managed to interrupt what she was saying by remarking dryly:

"You are making a mistake, Maureen. This is Miss . . ."

Even as he began to introduce Dorina she turned swiftly from the window where she had been standing and walking across the room went out through the door which Lady Maureen had left open when she entered.

"Wait!" the Earl tried to say.

But Lady Maureen's arms were around his neck, and she was saying with her crimson lips close against his:

"Dearest Oscar, do not be such a bore! I can assure you that you will find the country bumpkins very dull, but if you come back to London with me I will make sure you are amused and entranced by everything we do together."

She spoke very beguilingly, but the Earl said firmly with a note of anger in his voice:

"I have told you, Maureen, that I am not coming to London until I have had time to explore my new possessions, and I have already discovered that there is a lot for me to do here."

Lady Maureen shrugged her shoulders prettily and said:

"Then do not blame me if you are bored to distraction, which you will be. But, Oscar, I shall be bored too, without you!"

The Earl was about to reply when a man appeared in the doorway saying:

"Do come on, Maureen! The horses are restless and so, for that matter, am I!"

"I am coming Jarvis," Lady Maureen replied. "I was just trying to persuade your cousin to change his mind and come to London."

"I exhausted all the arguments about that last night," Jarvis replied. "I am sure Oscar will soon get bored when he finds that nothing ever happens in the country from one year's end to another. Then he will come post haste to London."

He looked at the Earl as he spoke in a provocative manner. At the same time he seemed to be almost pleading with him.

He was a quite good-looking young man.

At the same time, the Earl thought as he had thought before, he was over-dressed, almost to the point of being a Dandy, and he had the idea that he spent far too much on his clothes.

He was also convinced that he spent far too much money in a great many other ways.

As Jarvis Yarde opened the door wider, he said:

"I hope, Oscar, you have enjoyed your first house-party. I hate leaving you, but I have promised to take Maureen back to London. There is a party tomorrow night that neither of us wants to miss."

He paused for a moment before he added:

"Change your mind and come with us! I assure you it will be something you will not regret."

"I have made my plans," the Earl said quietly. "As I have already told you, Jarvis, there is so much for me to see to here, that for the moment I have no time for any more parties."

"You would have time for me," Lady Maureen said softly. "You must admit that, dearest Oscar."

Once again the Earl disentangled himself from the arms she was entwining around him and he said:

"You heard Jarvis say the horses were restless, and I expect those who are going with you are feeling restless too."

"He is right," Jarvis agreed. "Come on, Maureen,

there is no use hanging about."

Lady Maureen kissed the Earl passionately before she said softly:

"Goodbye, dearest, wonderful Oscar. I shall be thinking of you every minute and will be devastatingly lonely until you are with me again!"

The Earl took her by the arm and drew her firmly down the room and out along the passage towards the hall.

A few other guests were waiting for them there, and as he looked at the dissolute face of Sir Roger Chatham, who was one of Jarvis's friends and had been specially invited by him to Yarde, he had a suspicion that he might be the man who had assaulted the young housemaid the previous night, and brought the wrath of the Vicar's daughter down upon his head.

He thought Sir Roger was a man he could never like and would never trust.

It was only on Jarvis's insistence that he was an excellent fellow and an extremely good card-player that he had been invited to Yarde.

"If, in fact, it was he who assaulted the girl," the Earl told himself, "this is the last time he ever darkens any door of mine!"

As, however, he had no idea of making a scene, he merely said goodbye to Sir Roger politely and to the other members of the house-party who were waiting to bid him farewell.

Lady Maureen had the last word.

"If you have not come to London by the end of the week, Oscar, I shall make Jarvis bring me back to you," she said. "You know it is impossible for me to live without you."

The Earl murmured some noncommittal reply, helped Lady Maureen into the Phaeton which his

42

Cousin was driving, and before she could say any more he turned to help two other ladies, Sir Roger, and another man into a travelling-chariot.

They set off with shouts of goodbye and thanks for a very enjoyable party.

Only when the horses were moving down the drive did the Earl turn to find his one remaining guest, Harry Harringdon, standing beside him.

"Well, thank God that is over!" he exclaimed.

"I thought you were feeling like that," Harry said. "Another time you want to give a party, I suggest you choose your own guests rather than let Jarvis choose them for you."

"That is what I was thinking," the Earl replied, "and I have no liking for Chatham."

"Nor have I," Harry agreed, "a nasty piece of work! I have heard some rather unpleasant stories about him."

"What sort of stories?" the Earl asked sharply.

Harry Harringdon paused for a moment. Then he said:

"Oh – the usual vices that you and I find revolting! A penchant for very young girls, and that sort of thing."

The Earl's lips tightened before he said angrily:

"Why the hell did you not tell me?"

His friend looked at him in surprise.

"I had no chance to do so. Anyway, what was the point when the man was already your guest?"

"The sort of guest I do not intend to have again," the Earl said. "There is something else, Harry, that I have to check on. Wait for me in the Library. I will not be long."

"It will give me a chance to catch up on the newspapers," Harry said cheerfully and walked away in the direction of the Library.

43

He and the Earl had been at School together, and they had joined their Regiment on the same day.

The Earl had pulled strings with the Duke of Wellington to ensure that Harry stayed in France with the Army of Occupation when he did so, and they had enjoyed Paris together.

As Harry had said when it was time to go home:

"Enough is enough! I have had a surfeit of *pâté de foie gras* and shall be glad to return to roast beef and apple-pie."

"So shall I," the Earl had said, "and as I shall have a great deal to do in England, I shall need your help, Harry."

"To hear is to obey, Oh Master!" Harry had laughed.

The Earl knew that Harry would do anything for him he wanted, and he thought now that he would tell Harry everything the Vicar's daughter had said to him and see what he made of it.

As Harry disappeared towards the Library he looked round the hall and realised that Carter, the Butler, had not been there to see the guests leave.

He thought it rather strange and he said to one of the footmen:

"Where is Carter?"

There was a pause before the footman replied rather reluctantly:

"I think, M'Lord, Mr. Carter's restin'."

"Resting?" the Earl exclaimed. "At this time of the day?"

Instinctively he glanced at the large grandfather clock at the bottom of the stairs.

He spoke curtly as he said to the footman:

"Find Carter wherever he may be and say I want to speak to him!"

44

"I expect he's in the Pantry, M'Lord," the footman murmured.

"Never mind, I will find him myself," the Earl said. "You stay here on duty."

He walked away, moving through the hall into the long passage which led to the servants' quarters.

He was well aware that after luncheon in the Dining-Room the Butler usually had some time off. But that was no excuse for Carter not being in the hall when his guests were leaving.

The Earl was also thinking that the waiting at meals had not been as well performed as he would have expected, and that could only be the fault of the Butler whom Major Richardson had engaged for him.

He decided that after all Miss Stanfield had told him he would speak with Richardson first and find out why he had sacked the older servants in what was obviously considered an arbitrary and unjust manner, although he felt certain Richardson must have had his reasons.

Richardson was an Officer in another Regiment which was returning to England to be disbanded, and vaguely, at the back of his mind, he remembered when he engaged him as his Manager, he had asked him:

"What exactly do you want me to do, My Lord, until you arrive?"

"It is difficult for me to answer that question," the Earl had replied, "as I have never been to Yarde. But I understand my uncle was an old man when he died, so things must have become pretty slack. Do what you can to bring them up to date and bring a little youth and vitality into what I expect has become something of an old people's home!"

He had laughed as he spoke, but now he suspected that perhaps Richardson had taken him too literally.

"I must find out exactly what has happened," he

45

told himself and realised he was passing the Manager's office on his way to the kitchen-quarters.

He opened the door to stand transfixed at the scene that greeted him.

Richardson, who had been a good-looking soldier with a Cavalry type moustache, was lying back in a comfortable armchair in front of the fireplace.

Sitting on his knee was a large, blowzy woman whom the Earl recognised as having spoken to him in one of the upstairs passages to introduce herself as the Housekeeper.

She had one arm round the Manager's neck and opposite them in another chair was Carter, the Butler, in his shirt-sleeves, his tail-coat thrown carelessly on the floor beside him.

They were, all three of them, holding glasses in their hands, and there was an empty bottle of claret on the desk and another that was only a quarter full.

The Earl knew that it was the best claret which they had drunk at luncheon which together with his disgust at the scene before him, added insult to injury.

For a moment he just stood in the doorway staring as if he could hardly believe his eyes.

Then Major Richardson said in what was undoubtedly a slurred voice:

"D'you want me, M'Lord?"

As he spoke he made an effort to rise from the armchair, unbalancing as he did so the woman on his knee so that she upset the glass of claret she held in her hand over her gown.

"Be careful what you're doing!" she shrieked in a vulgar manner.

The Earl walked a little further into the room. Then as Carter got unsteadily to his feet, he said:

"Do not trouble to move! You will all leave this

46

house and my employment within the next two hours, without either a reference or wages!"

He turned as he spoke, then left the room closing the door quietly behind him.

Then, as he walked back along the passage towards the hall, he asked himself how he could have been such a fool to have made his first visit to Yarde with a large house-party which had prevented him from finding out what had been happening before he took over his inheritance.

. . . .

Dorina was putting away the tea-things as her father left the Dining-Room and the children were eating the last piece of cake.

"I expect you have some homework to do, Rosabelle," she said to her sister, "and I know Peter has."

"I am bored with homework!" Rosabelle protested. "I have been studying with Miss Soames the most boring subjects, and now I want to enjoy myself!"

"I know, dearest," Dorina replied sympathetically, "but you know as well as I do that Miss Soames cannot teach you in the few hours you are with her, all you have to learn."

"If you ask me, I do not think she is a very good teacher," Rosabelle said.

"She is the best in the village, and the only one we can afford," Dorina replied.

She spoke with a note of despair in her voice because she had thought for a long time that Rosabelle had learned almost everything Miss Soames could teach her, and that really she needed much more experienced Governesses for all she still had to learn.

She had tried to persuade her father to give Rosabelle some lessons, but while he had promised to do so, he always forgot, or else was so immersed in cataloguing and looking up the history of his cacti that he would forget what lesson he was supposed to be teaching her and in consequence they just talked together.

The same applied to Peter, although as far as he was concerned they had been fortunate enough to find a retired Don from Oxford who lived in the next village.

Because he was bored at having so little to do and was genuinely fond of the Vicar, he had agreed to teach Peter for a ridiculously small sum. Peter in consequence was for his age well educated.

At the same time, Dorina was sure there were a great many subjects that a younger man would be able to teach better than a man of over seventy.

She suspected the Professor was not sufficiently up to date in many of the subjects that Peter required if he was ever to go to a Public School.

"How can we ever afford it?" she asked herself night after night, and she would lie awake for hours trying to think of some practical way by which she could make money.

Sometimes she imagined that one of her father's cacti was so original and unusual that collectors would pay large sums of money to acquire it.

At other times she told herself that hidden somewhere in the attic of the old Vicarage was a picture, which, disguised by age and dirt, was really a masterpiece worth a fortune.

When morning came she was always back to facing the unpalatable truth that she had only a few shillings to spend for the rest of the month, while the bills had added up to what would take half of next month's housekeeping allowance.

"What can we do?" Dorina would ask a million times, only to find there was no answer to her problem.

Rosabelle, having eaten the last morsel of cake, said:

"I hope you have something nice for supper, Dorina, because to be truthful, I am still hungry."

"So am I!" Peter said. "If you ask me, we had a very mingy tea!"

"I am sorry, darlings," Dorina replied, "I will try to find something nice for you for tonight."

She spoke optimistically, but she had an uncomfortable feeling that the larder was bare and Nanny would say firmly that they would have to make do, mostly with potatoes and a few greens from the garden.

"We cannot go on like this!" Dorina told herself.

At that moment Rosabelle, who had walked into the Hall, gave a scream of excitement and came flying back into the Dining-Room.

"Dorina!" she exclaimed. "There is a Phaeton outside which is smarter than anything we have ever seen, and a gentleman, I know it is the Earl, is getting down from it. He has come to call on us – he has, really!"

For a moment Dorina was still. Then she said:

"Go and do your homework, Rosabelle, and do not tell Papa that His Lordship is here. I want to speak to him alone."

"Why? What are you going to say to him?" Rosabelle enquired.

"That is my business!" Dorina answered. "Just do as I tell you!"

"But I want to see him, I want to meet him!" Rosabelle protested.

Because Nanny was out and there was no one else to answer the knock on the front door, Dorina was obliged to do so herself.

When she opened it she saw the Earl standing outside

looking exceedingly smart, and as he lifted his tall hat from his dark head she could not help being aware that he was also very good-looking.

"Good-afternoon, Miss Stanfield. I would like to come in and talk to you, if you are not too busy."

"I have very little time, My Lord," Dorina said coldly after she had curtsied, "but please, come in."

Rosabelle who had been standing in the background ran forward.

"I know you are the new Earl!" she said eagerly. "I saw you this morning riding in the Park on the most magnificent stallion!"

"Rosabelle!" Dorina said sharply, then to the Earl: "I apologise, My Lord, that my sister and brother have been in the Park without your permission. But it was something they were always allowed to do in the past."

"Please," Rosabelle pleaded before the Earl could speak, "may we go there now? It is miserable just to walk about in the village when we would much rather be in your beautiful, beautiful woods."

"I am delighted for you to go there whenever you wish," the Earl replied.

Rosabelle gave a cry of delight.

"I hoped you would say that, but Dorina was very strict with us and said we were not to impose on you."

"I assure you, you are not imposing in the slightest," the Earl replied.

"Thank you, oh, thank you!" Rosabelle beamed. "I think you are very kind – and a wonderful rider!"

"I would like to see your stallion too," a voice said from the staircase and before Dorina could stop him, Peter came running into the hall.

"When the last Earl was alive," he said, "Old Hawkins used to let me help him with the horses. He said I was better than any of the stable-lads and a great help to him, but Dorina will not let me go there now."

The Earl glanced at Dorina with a touch of amusement in his eyes.

"I feel," he said, "that your sister has been somewhat unfriendly. If you were waiting for my permission please go to the stables as often as you like. I am sure you will not do anything to upset my grooms."

"No, of course not!" Peter cried, "and thank you, thank you very much!"

"And now," Dorina said severely, "as His Lordship is in a hurry, will you please go upstairs and do your homework?"

"It will not seem so dull now that I can go in the Park," Rosabelle said irrepressibly.

Dorina led the way into the Drawing-Room and the Earl followed her, aware as he did so that while she was still extremely incensed with him, at the same time she was undoubtedly one of the prettiest young women he had ever seen in his life.

Without the unbecoming, plain bonnet she had worn when she called on him this morning, she was wearing a cotton gown which, because it had been washed many times and in consequence had shrunk, revealed the perfection of her figure.

He thought as she went to the end of the room and turned to face him that with her golden hair and grey eyes she looked like a young goddess who had stepped down from Olympus to take human shape and bemuse the human beings.

Then he told himself he was being very fanciful in what was undoubtedly an uncomfortable situation.

"May I say, before we start talking seriously, Miss Stanfield," he began, "how charming I find your sister

51

and brother? The former will doubtless in a few years be a beauty!"

"You mean to be kind to them, My Lord," Dorina replied, "but I feel, for reasons I would rather not express, that it would be best for them not to be involved in any way with Your Lordship."

The Earl seated himself in an armchair without being invited to do so and said:

"Because I find it rather exhausting to keep fighting with you all the time, Miss Stanfield, let me say at once that I have already learnt that you were quite right in everything you said to me. I can only apologise humbly for doubting what came as a complete surprise to me."

Dorina's eyes widened and he knew she was astonished that he should apologise so fully. Then before she could speak he went on:

"I am sure you will be glad to hear that I have summarily dismissed Major Richardson and the woman whom he had appointed as Housekeeper, and the Butler whose name was Carter was dismissed with them. They had all left Yarde before I came here!"

"I am glad .. very glad!" Dorina said breathlessly.

"Now that I have depleted my household, Miss Stanfield, I can only look to you to replace them as quickly as possible."

Dorina stared at him as if she could hardly believe what she had heard. Then she said:

"Are .. are you really .. suggesting that I should .. find you the people you should employ, My Lord?"

"Unless you do so, I have no idea where I shall find replacements," the Earl answered.

Dorina pressed her hands together.

"I know Burrows the old Butler would be thrilled to go back, and I am sure you can persuade Mrs.

Meadows, although she is rather bitter about the way in which she was treated."

"I do not think it is a question of *my* persuading her! As you are aware, I am a stranger, and I do not know how I can fill the gaps that have been caused by your revelations which so unfortunately were true!"

Dorina drew in her breath.

"I can tell you in which cottages Burrows and Mrs. Meadows live."

"I think it would make things very much easier," the Earl said, "if you would come with me and introduce me to two people who I am well aware know a great deal more about my house than I know myself."

Dorina stared at him.

"Do you really .. mean that?"

"As it happens, I never say things I do not mean," the Earl said, "and to save my own face I would like to claim I am not often as mistaken about somebody's character as I was about Richardson. I read his credentials provided by his Commanding Officer and they were very impressive. But I suppose I made a mistake in thinking that a good soldier would make a good Manager. I was wrong, and therefore you must forgive me. That, surely, would be the Christian thing to do?"

Dorina, who had been staring at him as if mesmerised, looked away.

"I .. I think, My Lord, you are laughing at me!"

"Not really," the Earl said quietly. "I came here to apologise, and also I have a great desire to put things right."

"Then I shall be very glad to help you, My Lord!"

She spoke eagerly. At the same time, the Earl was aware from the expression in her eyes that while she was glad of his change of heart, she was still condemning him and was in a way, wary of him.

He could not explain how he knew this except that to him her eyes were very revealing, and although she was young and quite obviously inexperienced in the world, she had an undeniable personality which it was impossible to ignore.

He had the strange feeling that he could read her thoughts, and he was certain that, while she accepted the olive branch, where it concerned Yarde, she was still suspicious of him and, although he disliked the word, disapproving.

He suspected that this sprang from her meeting with Lady Maureen, and he told himself that if he was to reinstate himself in Miss Stanfield's eyes and through her win over the village and the employees, he would have to tread very carefully.

"What I suggest, Miss Stanfield," he said, "is that you come with me now in my Phaeton, and we persuade the two people who Richardson dismissed to come back to Yarde as quickly as possible. At least then I shall have a Housekeeper and a Butler!"

"It is very important that you should have them back, My Lord," Dorina said. "You will understand that in sending them away at a moment's notice without any compensation after years of faithful service, your action has created a very unfortunate feeling among all the others who work for you."

She paused for breath, then went on:

"What is more, Carter the new Butler, engaged as footmen the worst boys in the village whose families have only recently moved here and are not yet accepted by those who have lived in Little Sodbury all their lives."

She spoke so seriously that the Earl could not help saying as his eyes twinkled:

"I find it extraordinary, Miss Stanfield, that you,

54

looking so attractive, have not far more important interests of your own to occupy your mind than these petty domestic difficulties of mine. After all, Yarde is not really your concern."

"Perhaps you are unaware of the fact that my father is your incumbent, My Lord," Dorina said, "and we are therefore extremely concerned as to what sort of person you are, and if we can continue to count on your patronage."

As she spoke the Earl realised he had not understood although of course he should have, that the Vicar of the Parish in which he lived was most probably appointed by him, and that he could, if he wished, dismiss him as any other of his servants could be dismissed.

Once again, he thought a little ruefully that he had made a mistake where Dorina was concerned.

But he merely said quickly:

"I feel, Miss Stanfield, that we will have plenty of time to discuss all these matters, and of course I shall depend on you to explain to me many things that bewilder me at the moment. But one thing at a time, and let us start with my Butler and Housekeeper."

Dorina held her chin high and walking towards the door she said:

"I will put on my bonnet, My Lord. I will not keep you waiting."

"Thank you," the Earl said gravely.

When he was alone he thought with amusement that this was perhaps the first time in his life that he had been with a pretty woman who spoke to him with ice in her voice.

And whatever answer in words she gave to anything he said, he could see an expression of condemnation and what he was certain was containing dislike in her eyes.

CHAPTER THREE

Dorina thought that even the Earl, insensitive and obtuse as she still thought him to be, could not fail to see how despondent old Burrows looked when they called at his cottage.

Several slates were missing on the roof, the windows were cracked, and it must have been years since anyone had painted the woodwork.

When the old man opened the door his eyes lit up for a moment when he saw Dorina.

"Oh, it's you, Miss Dorina!" he said. "Come in, though I'm ashamed to ask you into such a hovel as I've ever lived in!"

He then saw that Dorina was not alone and he stood for a moment staring at the Earl who put out his hand and said:

"I have asked Miss Stanfield to bring me here to apologise to you for the way in which you have been treated, which I want to say firmly was not on my orders."

Old Burrows gasped, then he said:

"Will Your Lordship come in? And be careful o' the flags on the floor, as they're very uneven."

When the Earl was inside the cottage and saw how

sparsely furnished it was and lacking in comforts, Dorina thought he must be aware of how humiliating it was for a man who had long been of Burrows' importance to be treated in such a manner.

She could not help appreciating the direct way the Earl without any palaver sat down on a chair and said:

"I have come to ask you, Burrows, to come back immediately to Yarde and restore it to order. I am afraid you will find that things have deteriorated badly since you left, and Miss Stanfield tells me the new footmen should not have been engaged in the first place. I shall look to you to replace them and make everything as it was in my uncle's day."

Burrows drew in his breath.

"All I can say, M'Lord, is that I can only do my best."

"Thank you," the Earl said, "and as Miss Stanfield and I are now calling to see Mrs. Meadows, I suggest that as soon as I return home, I will send a carriage to bring you both back to Yarde, which you should never have left."

It seemed to Dorina that Burrows became ten years younger as the Earl spoke.

He appeared to grow taller and straighter, and it was as if a magic wand had transformed him back into the man he had been before the old Earl died.

They left and drove onto the end of the village towards the cottage of Mrs. Meadows.

Dorina was aware that the Earl was smiling, and after a moment when she did not speak he said:

"Can I have done something wrong again, or are you so ungenerous as not to commend me?"

"I think once again, My Lord, you are laughing at me," Dorina replied, "but you have made Burrows very happy, so of course I am grateful."

She did not really sound very grateful, and the Earl suspected she was being deliberately uneffusive because she had been shocked at the way Lady Maureen had behaved.

He found it hard to believe that was the reason, and yet he was afraid that Dorina was looking on him as a Rake and Roué and, although it was extremely unfair, connecting him in her mind with the guest who had assaulted the young housemaid.

They drove on in silence until when they came to an even more dilapidated cottage than the one in which Burrows had been put, the Earl knew that Dorina perhaps subconsciously was hoping he would notice it and all the other cottages in the village that needed repairing.

As if he had asked the question aloud she said a little reluctantly:

"When your uncle was ill everything was neglected because there was no one to give orders, and also the war had made everything so expensive that even at Yarde there had to be strict economies."

The Earl did not say anything, he merely handed the reins once again to his groom who had jumped down from behind, then helped Dorina to alight.

Mrs. Meadows opened the door when they knocked and once again the Earl saw her face light up when she saw Dorina.

Then, as she realised who was with her, she stiffened and dropped the Earl a curtsy that in itself expressed her feelings.

Once again he held out his hand and said:

"I have come, Mrs. Meadows, to offer you an apology for the way you were sent away from Yarde, and I am begging you to come back immediately and put a great many things right which have gone wrong in your absence."

Instead of the delight which Burrows had shown at such a humble invitation Mrs. Meadows merely replied:

"I thank Your Lordship, but after the way I was insulted by your Manager and turned out of the place I had always looked on as my home for thirty years, I would not think of returning."

The Earl gave Dorina a look of consternation, and she moved a step forward to put her hand on Mrs. Meadows' arm.

"I have a suspicion," she said in a low voice, "that you know already of the terrible things that have been happening at Yarde, which would have shocked and horrified the old Earl, and greatly distressed Mama. Please, Mrs. Meadows, come back and put things right. There is no one else, and you cannot allow things to go on as they are."

For a moment Mrs. Meadows did not speak and the Earl thought she was once again going to refuse.

Then she looked at Dorina's pleading eyes and said sharply:

"I couldn't believe my ears, Miss Dorina, when I was told what had happened to Mary Bell. Your dear mother would turn over in her grave, God rest her soul, if she knew about it!"

"Such things must not happen again," Dorina said in a low voice.

Mrs. Meadows looked at the Earl and she said:

"I'll come back, M'Lord, only on condition that if anything like that occurs again I can inform you immediately and Your Lordship'll support me whoever is concerned."

The way she spoke made both Dorina and the Earl aware that the story of the behaviour of his guests, and not only that which concerned Mary Bell, had deeply

59

shocked her and she was, although it seemed extraordinary, not at all anxious to return to Yarde in such circumstances.

"You have my assurance," the Earl said quietly, "that the unfortunate incident that occurred last night will not be repeated. But I am afraid, Mrs. Meadows, that the young people of today do not have the dignity or the good manners of their elders."

It was what Mrs. Meadows thought herself, and Dorina knew the Earl had won the battle.

But Mrs. Meadows had the last word.

"I'm hoping, M'Lord," she said, "that everything your family has stood for all the years I've been in service will continue to set an example not only here on the Estate, but where, M'Lord, it's very much needed, in London!"

The Earl was surprised but realised that the stories of the behaviour of the Prince Regent and the Society that followed his lead had not gone unrepeated, even in Little Sodbury.

Mrs. Meadows turned again to Dorina.

"I hopes, Miss Dorina," she said, "that you'll never forget that your mother set an example to the whole village with her kindness and her understanding. She were good from the top of her head to the soles of her feet, bless her, and she was everything a Yarde should be."

Dorina was aware that Mrs. Meadows was in her own way preaching at the Earl, and she realised that when she said her mother was a Yarde he looked surprised.

As she expected, as soon as they drove away from Mrs. Meadows' cottage promising that the carriage would fetch her at the same time as Burrows to take them back to the Big House, the Earl said:

"Why did you not tell me that your mother was one of my relations?"

"Hers was a different branch of the family from yours," Dorina answered.

"Nevertheless, a cousin!"

"Several times removed but, as you say, a cousin!"

"Seeing that we both have the same blood running in our veins," the Earl said, "it is obviously your bounden duty to help me. What do you suggest I do next?"

It flashed through Dorina's mind that he was teasing her.

Then she thought perhaps he was serious and this was, of course, an opportunity that she should not miss.

She longed to say that she hoped he would help her father by increasing his stipend.

Then she knew that in view of her still persisting dislike for him, it was impossible for her to ask such a thing.

But Rosabelle said it for her.

When they drove back to the Vicarage the Earl said:

"I think now I should meet your father, if he is at home."

"Papa will probably be in the garden," Dorina replied, "but perhaps, as you have to arrange for a carriage to pick up Mrs. Meadows and Burrows, you could wait to meet him another day?"

"I feel it is something I should do now," the Earl said firmly, and she was aware there was no use in arguing with him.

She therefore went into the house, the Earl following her, and directing him into the Drawing-Room she said:

"If you will wait here, I will fetch Papa."

"I would like to come with you," the Earl said, "but as I realise you have no wish for my company, I will do as you suggest."

Dorina went out of the room with what was almost a flounce which, although she was not aware of it, made the Earl want to laugh.

He found it a new experience not only to be looked on with dislike by a very pretty woman, but also to realise that he was having to use considerable pressure to make her do what he wished.

He knew that with every instinct in her body she longed to send him away and refuse to have anything at all to do with him.

"She is shocked by what has happened," he told himself, "and who shall blame her? At the same time, she is the one person available to help me, and it is really rather tiresome that she cannot forgive and forget."

The door opened and he thought it would admit Dorina and her father, but it was Rosabelle.

She advanced towards him and he thought that with her fair hair and blue eyes she was the prettiest child he had seen for years.

"I saw you arriving from my bedroom window, when I was doing my homework," she said, "and I came down to talk to you."

"It is very kind of you," the Earl replied. "Your sister would not let me go with her into the garden to find your father."

"I expect she wants to tidy him up before he meets you," Rosabelle said, "but I want to thank you for saying I could go in the Park and in the woods."

"You have already thanked me," the Earl replied, "and I hope you will come to visit me at Yarde. I am sure you as a family know a great deal more about it than I do."

"It is a beautiful house!" Rosabelle said. "We often would go there for tea or luncheon with your uncle

62

until he became too ill, and we always had delicious food!"

"I hope that is what I can offer you in the future," the Earl smiled.

"We had gorgeous iced cakes for tea," Rosabelle went on, "and dishes for luncheon that we have never been able to afford."

She gave a little sigh and added:

"All we have is rabbit and more rabbit! I am sure my ears are growing longer until one day they will stand up on my head and I expect too I shall grow a small fluffy tail!"

The Earl laughed.

"A very sad story!"

"I know," Rosabelle agreed, "but now Mama is dead, we never really have enough to eat."

The Earl stared at her in astonishment.

"I cannot believe that is true!"

"You ask Nanny," Rosabelle said. "She will tell you it is a crying shame and a disgrace that we should have to live on so little, with the tradesmen refusing to give us any more goods until we can pay our bills."

The Earl remembered that Dorina had said that the living was his, and he supposed this was another complaint that would be laid eventually at his door.

He thought, however, that Rosabelle was probably exaggerating, and he was not surprised when Dorina returned with the Vicar that she immediately sent her back to finish her homework.

The Vicar had obviously brushed his hair and washed his hands before coming to meet his guest, and remembering what Rosabelle had said the Earl could not help noticing how thin all the family were, while the Vicar looked almost gaunt.

He was wondering whether he should refer to the matter of the stipend right away when the Vicar said:

"I am afraid I cannot offer you what you would feel was adequate refreshment, My Lord, but perhaps you would like a cup of tea?"

"Thank you," the Earl replied. "I find myself quite thirsty after all the talking your daughter and I have had to do to persuade Mrs. Meadows and Burrows to come back to Yarde."

"You are having them both back?" the Vicar asked. "Good! It was a great mistake that they were sent away in the first place!"

Dorina left the room to see to the tea, and leaning forward in his chair the Earl said:

"I need the help, Vicar, of both you and your family. Because I have taken a year in which to return, I understand that a great many things have been changed for the worse by the man I put in charge as Manager, and which I now know was a great mistake."

"You mean Richardson?" the Vicar said. "I agree with you. He has got the whole village up in arms against him, and if you had not mentioned it, I would have thought it my duty to tell you what has been occurring in your absence."

"I have learnt that already and Richardson has been dismissed."

"You have dismissed him?" the Vicar repeated. "That is excellent news indeed – excellent!"

He told the Earl how worried he had been about the farmers having their rents increased, and how one family who had been farming on the estate for two generations had been given notice to quit in a month's time.

The Earl made a note of their name and said:

"You are telling me exactly what I want to know,

Vicar, and these things will be rectified and there is really no one to whom I can turn for help and advice except yourself. I understand moreover that your wife was a relative of mine."

"Yes, she was a Yarde," the Vicar agreed, "and although her family did not wish her to marry me, we were very happy and I miss her more than I can ever express in words."

It was easy after that for the Earl to ask whether there were any other livings of which he was the Patron.

He learnt there were five, although two parishes were at the moment without incumbents and the Bishop was waiting his return so that he could interview the applicants.

"There is one thing I want to know," the Earl said, "for I imagine that like everything else since the war your expenses have increased while your stipend has remained static."

"That is true," the Vicar agreed.

A number of questions tactfully put by the Earl eventually revealed that the Vicar's income was hopelessly inadequate for the needs of the Vicarage and for the family.

There also had to be included those who came to him for help in times of distress, and whom he felt it impossible to send away empty-handed.

"My wife had an allowance during her lifetime," the Vicar said, "which was discontinued on her death. Her father had left her this in his will, but because he disliked me, and was angry that being so beautiful she had not made a better marriage, the income from the capital is to be paid to the children only after they have reached the age of twenty-one, and I am unable to draw from it even on their behalf in the meantime."

"I think your daughter Dorina must take after her mother," the Earl remarked.

"That is true," the Vicar agreed. "My wife was a very beautiful Yarde and Dorina is almost a replica of her. Rosabelle has, however, inherited, as I expect you have noticed, the blue eyes and fair hair that run in my family because somewhere far back in our ancestry we had Viking blood in us."

The Earl was interested and would have enquired further, when Rosabelle reappeared to say that Dorina had sent her to tell them that tea was ready.

They went into the Dining-Room and Peter joined them from upstairs, eager to talk to the Earl about his horses.

As they sat down at the table where everything was laid out on a clean cloth, the Earl realised from the very little there was to eat that Rosabelle's story of starvation was not exaggerated.

There were a few neatly arranged sandwiches which he was sure Dorina had cut quickly when he had said he would stay for tea.

There were the remains of a cottage loaf, a small pat of butter, and some plum jam in a glass dish.

Dorina said nothing, but the Earl was aware that Rosabelle made a grimace when Peter passed the jam to her and he remembered when he was a boy disliking plums simply because there was such a profusion of them growing at Yarde.

The Vicar, however, noticed nothing. He ate a sandwich absent-mindedly, talking to the Earl about the farmers on the estate and the lamentable fact that there was very little work for the young men of the village.

"I cannot help feeling, My Lord," he said, "that if you could see your way to cut down some of the trees in the woods which are badly overgrown, or perhaps to open up one of the old gravel-pits which have been closed for the last ten years, it would give the boys growing up as well as their fathers, something better to do than lounging about on the village green hoping they might have a chance of holding a stranger's horse if he called at *The Green Dragon*.

"I shall certainly consider it," the Earl said. "Do you think it a good idea, Miss Stanfield?"

He deliberately spoke to Dorina who had been sitting at the top of the table pouring out the tea and making no effort to join in the conversation.

"I think it an excellent idea, My Lord," she replied, "if you are really considering doing something. But of course, you may be too busy with your parties in London, in which case it would be a great mistake to raise everybody's hopes only to have them disappointed."

The Earl realised she was once again doing battle with him and he replied:

"I understand what you are saying, Miss Stanfield, and I think it would be a good idea if you and your father could show me on a map those parts of the estate and the woods which you think need attention, and the actual site of the gravel pits. As you are aware, I am a stranger to Yarde, and have not yet found my way about."

He was amused as he realised that, strangely, he could read Dorina's thoughts, and she was trying frantically to think of somebody else who could advise him rather than her father or herself.

Apparently no one came to mind, and he said after a moment:

"Another thing we should consider as soon as possible, is who we should appoint as Estate Manager in Richardson's place. I intend to take a very active interest in what is going on, but I shall also need a Manager under me to carry out my orders."

"I wish I was old enough to do it!" Peter said. "Then I could ride your horses."

"I think we might discuss your doing that," the Earl replied. "At the same time I am afraid you will have to wait a few years and, of course, make a success of your schooling before I can appoint you to such an important position."

He realised that Peter was looking at him with an air of expectancy and excitement and he added:

"Will you come up to the house tomorrow? You can show me the stables and perhaps we can find a horse you can ride when you are not too busy with your lessons."

Peter gave a cry of sheer excitement and because it was difficult for him to express what he was feeling in words, the Vicar said:

"That is exceedingly kind of you, My Lord, but I could not allow my children to be a nuisance to you."

"I assure you they will not be that," the Earl replied.

"If Peter is coming to the Big House tomorrow, can I come too?" Rosabelle asked.

"You will have to ask your sister," the Earl replied, "but I expect it can be arranged."

"In the meantime there will be no treats of that sort," Dorina said sharply, "if your homework is not finished."

Immediately Rosabelle and Peter left the Dining-Room and ran upstairs.

When they had gone the Vicar also went to his Study to find an old map of the estate which he told the Earl would show the place where the gravel pits had been worked for hundreds of years.

68

That left the Earl and Dorina alone in the Dining-Room and as he rose to his feet she rose too.

"I want to speak to you, My Lord."

"I am listening," he said.

"I know you are trying to be kind, and I think too you are trying to make reparation for what has occurred in your absence, but please, and do not think I am being rude when I ask you not to encourage Rosabelle to come to your house."

She did not look at him as she spoke, but he saw the faint colour come into her cheeks.

For a moment there was silence. Then he said:

"I know exactly what you are thinking, Miss Stanfield – perhaps as I now find we are related I should say 'Dorina'. But there is no possible chance of Rosabelle encountering the type of man that was by chance staying with me these last few days, and I assure you he will not be asked again!"

"But .. there are .. other men," Dorina said in a very quiet voice.

"Of course!" the Earl agreed. "But they will be my personal friends and, I can promise you, of no danger to anyone so young as Rosabelle."

He hoped from the sincere way he tried to speak that Dorina would respond, but instead to his surprise she said:

"I am sorry, but I still think it would be a .. mistake for Rosabelle to be involved with your .. friends."

She hesitated over the last word and the Earl thought that she was referring to Lady Maureen. Then his instinct told him it was more than that and after a moment he said:

"Suppose, Dorina, you make yourself a little plainer. What are you really driving at? Whom are you afraid of your sister meeting? Unless of course, as you have

69

such a dislike of me you are afraid that I might hurt her."

He was being, he thought, almost brutally frank in what he said, but he wanted to startle Dorina into telling him the truth.

There was a little pause when she looked at him, then looked away again.

"Tell me," he insisted, "what you are thinking."

Slowly, as if every word was dragged from her mouth reluctantly, she said after a moment:

"I do not wish Rosabelle to meet .. unless it is absolutely .. unavoidable .. your Cousin Jarvis."

The Earl was astonished. This was something he had not expected and after a moment he asked:

"May I ask why? You must have some good reason for what you have just said."

"I have .. no wish to give one, My Lord," Dorina said quickly, "and surely it cannot matter to you? My father and I are willing to be useful for the moment, but once you have everything in your own hands you will be able to manage very well without us."

"Perhaps you are right," the Earl said. "At the same time, as for the moment we are deeply involved with each other, I do not think you can cast aspersions against Jarvis Yarde, who is your cousin as well as mine, without substantiating what you have said."

"I see no reason why I should do so!" Dorina said crossly. "All I am asking is that you will help me where Rosabelle is concerned by keeping her away from your house, and most especially from those you will have staying with you."

"And if I refuse?" the Earl demanded.

Dorina drew in her breath, then she looked at him and he saw the anger in her eyes.

"For Heaven's sake!" he said. "What are we fighting

about, and why? I have apologised for the mistake I made in sending the wrong Manager to Yarde, and I have apologised for what occurred during the house-party of people who were not my friends, but acquaintances I had made when I first arrived in London."

"What you are saying is that they were friends of Cousin Jarvis!" Dorina said.

"I suppose that is true," the Earl agreed. "He certainly greeted me very effusively when I returned last week and was in fact the only member of the family to do so."

"That was, I am sure, because nobody expected you back, since you had not notified anyone of your arrival. There are dozens of Yardes who would have been only too thrilled to offer you their hospitality and assure you of their delight that you had at last returned to take up your duties as head of the family. But I expect Cousin Jarvis wanted you all to himself!"

The Earl looked at her speculatively.

"What has Jarvis done to upset you? Has he made advances to you?"

"Certainly not!" Dorina said sharply. "In fact, I doubt if he knows I exist. But I think, My Lord, you would .. be well advised to .. choose your .. friends very carefully in your .. new position."

She spoke hesitatingly, then said quickly:

"That is all I have to say! I am sorry that I cannot tell you any more."

She walked towards the door as she spoke and would have opened it if the Earl had not reached out first and prevented her from leaving the room.

"You can hardly expect me to be satisfied with that," he said. "Be sensible, Dorina! I am trying to find my way out of a maze, and instead of helping me you are making things very much more difficult."

"I am sorry you should think that," Dorina said. "At the same time, I have nothing more to add to what I have already said."

"And yet you are asking me to keep Rosabelle and Peter away from Yarde! Well, you have not made out at all a convincing case as to why I should do so, and until you do, I shall ignore your request, simply because it is unreasonable."

"It is not unreasonable!" Dorina contradicted. "Apart from anything else, you must realise that the way you live is very different from our way of life, and it would be a great mistake for the children to develop expensive tastes and expensive ideas which they will never be able to fulfil in their own lives."

"You cannot be sure of that," the Earl objected. "Moreover I have just been asking your father's help not only in getting to know the Parishes where I have the duty of appointing the incumbents but also of improving their position economically, which I understand is out of date with what is required of them at the moment."

Dorina's eyes widened.

"Are you saying in a somewhat roundabout way that you intend to increase their stipends?" she asked.

"Where your father is concerned I intend to do so at once," the Earl replied, "because I need his help with the other Parsons, and I suspect that the needs of each and every individual are different from the others."

For a moment Dorina could only stare at him. Then she said:

"If you really intend to help Papa financially, I can only say 'thank you' from the bottom of my heart!"

Despite her resolution to speak quietly and without emotion, tears came into her eyes and she turned away quickly, hoping the Earl had not seen them.

He did not say anything, he only opened the door and went out into the hall just as the Vicar came from the Study with a map in his hand.

. . . . . .

Ten minutes later the Earl was driving back to Yarde.

As he did so he was thinking of the very strange afternoon he had spent with Dorina and how much he had learned about his new possessions and the people he employed.

It seemed extraordinary that there was really no one to guide and advise him as to what was expected of him in his new position, except apparently for a young girl who condemned him for everything that had happened and for which he felt he was not entirely responsible.

Harry was waiting for him when he reached the Big House and although in his absence he had been reading, he asked somewhat petulantly:

"What has been keeping you? I thought you were going to join me, as we planned!"

"I have had quite a number of problems to deal with, Harry," the Earl said, "such as I never expected in my wildest dreams when I inherited the Earldom!"

"I am waiting to hear about them," Harry laughed, "but I do not expect they are insurmountable."

"I am not certain," the Earl replied, "but first, I want you to tell me what you know about Jarvis Yarde?"

"He is your cousin!"

"I am aware of that!" the Earl replied impatiently. "I am serious, Harry, so tell me the truth."

"Because as you are aware, I have been abroad for some time," Harry said, "what I have heard about your relative is mostly hearsay from friends in White's who all gossip."

"What did they tell you?"

Harry looked embarrassed.

"I do not want to make trouble."

"The only trouble you will be in," the Earl said sharply, "is if you are not frank with me, which is something you have always been in the past."

"Very well," Harry sighed, "if you want to know the truth, he is considered something of a bounder. He was exceedingly delighted when he learned you were returning from Paris to open Yarde House in Berkeley Square. As you must remember, he was your first visitor, and might almost be said to have been sitting on your doorstep waiting for your return."

"He seemed sincere," the Earl said.

"Of course," Harry agreed.

"What do you mean – of course?"

"You are the head of the family, old boy," Harry replied, "and to all intents and purposes a rich man. Jarvis, I understand, is in dire straits, and started borrowing money right and left even before your uncle's death, which he knew was imminent, and after he had heard of the death of Charles, on the chance that you would be killed in the last few weeks of the war. After that, when the French were no longer firing at us with bullets but with words he was not so cheerful."

"I do not know what the devil you are saying!" the Earl exclaimed. "How can Jarvis Yarde benefit by my death?"

"Either you are being extremely obtuse," Harry said, "or else you have not troubled to enquire, which is more likely, into the position in which you now find yourself."

"I am listening," the Earl said curtly. "Go on!"

"If you had looked closely into your family-tree, you

74

would have realised that Jarvis is your heir presumptive."

The Earl sat bolt upright.

"I do not believe it!"

"It is true! Just as you inherited rather as an outsider after both the direct heirs to the Earldom were killed, so, unless you produce a son, which is something I advise you to do quickly, Jarvis Yarde will become the 8th Earl of Yardcombe on your death!"

"And you say he is borrowing money on it?"

"As soon as your cousin Charles lost his life, Jarvis went to a Usurer and obtained not a very large sum, but enough for him to indulge his very unusual tastes in women for a few more months."

"Why did you not tell me?" the Earl asked.

"I think from the way he has been toadying to you ever since your return from Paris," Harry replied, "you can be quite certain, in fact I do not mind taking a bet on it, that he will try and touch you for a considerable sum of money within the next week or so."

"Then he will be disappointed!" the Earl said sharply. "I have no intention of settling the debts of my impecunious relations until I have calculated how much I have to expend on the estate and on the people I employ in one capacity or another."

"A very laudable statement!" Harry said mockingly. "But I warn you, Oscar, that Jarvis, from all I hear, is one of those insidious creatures who like an octopus, once he has wormed his way into your life, will enclose you and crush you with his tentacles until you find it impossible to be rid of him."

"I have never heard such a lot of nonsense," the Earl scoffed, "and I do not believe a word of it!"

He thought his friend was exaggerating.

At the same time he could remember all too vividly how he had compelled Dorina to tell him what she was thinking, and how there had been when she spoke of Jarvis Yarde an undoubted note of horror in her soft voice.

CHAPTER FOUR

When the Earl had left, Dorina went into the small Sitting-Room and sat down to look at her mother's portrait which hung over the mantelpiece.

It had been painted by a local artist soon after she was married, and although he was not very skilled in his profession, he had somehow caught the joy, happiness and sweetness that had always exuded from Mrs. Stanfield and which to other people had been infectious.

Dorina looked up at it, then she said beneath her breath:

"Should I have told him, Mama? I felt he would not believe me and would think I was making it up."

There was no answer, and Dorina sat thinking of the strange thing that had happened after the old Earl's Funeral.

A great number of Yardes had come to it, and it had been arranged that they should have luncheon at the Big House when the Funeral was over.

Most of them had come from some distance, and therefore, as soon as they had eaten and drunk and conversed briefly with relations they had not seen for years, they hurried away in their carriages, coaches and

Phaetons, so that sooner than Dorina had expected everybody had left.

She and her father had greeted everybody because they were the only Yardes who actually lived in Little Sodbury.

Dorina knew that if her mother had still been alive, she would have played hostess now that the two direct heirs to the title were dead and Oscar Yarde, the new Earl, was in France.

The Earl had died five months after Waterloo when hostilities had ceased.

Although there was much rejoicing now that peace had come, there was also a deep depression in England, not only over the men who had lost their lives in battle, but because of the financial difficulties which were besetting not only the farmers but almost everybody else.

Dorina knew that the old Earl had been glad to die. He was too ill to face the new problems of everyday life on his large estates, and having lost his two sons who had meant everything to him, he had no wish to go on living.

In the Church she found herself wondering what the new Earl would be like, and if he would be able to take his uncle's place and be as loved and respected as William would have been had he lived.

Then somehow, and she could not explain it to herself, she was suddenly and acutely aware of her Cousin Jarvis.

She did not know why, but she had always disliked him ever since they had met as children.

Since she had grown up, she had thought that he went out of his way to be condescending and often rude to her when they met.

He gave the impression that he sneered at her father

for being a Parson and considered him and his family unimportant because they were poor and of no social consequence.

She told herself she was being un-Christian, and yet when she looked at Jarvis, sitting just across the aisle from her in the front pew, she was sure that he was almost mocking the service, which was being taken by her father, and was somehow bringing a hostile attitude into the Church.

"It is ridiculous for me to feel like this!" she had told herself.

Yet she remembered that when she had a kind of intuition about people or a perception she was nearly always right.

She said goodbye to the last guest, an elderly cousin who had wept throughout the Funeral Service, but who as far as Dorina could remember, had not been to Yarde for at least ten years.

Now she told herself she could go home and went upstairs to the State Room in which she had left the black coat she had worn at the Funeral.

It was lying on the large four-poster bed which at luncheon-time had been heaped with the coats of the other guests, some of them being rich and expensive, others as poor and almost as threadbare as her own.

She picked it up thinking it was getting chilly now that the sun had gone down, and she would certainly need it as she walked home through the Park to the Vicarage.

Then she heard a strange sound which at first sounded like the buzzing of a bee, then it seemed to her something like an incantation.

She wondered what it could be and thought it came from a room not far away. But that seemed impossible as she was sure the guests had all gone.

79

Also the servants would by now have returned to the kitchen quarters doubtless to finish up what was left of the food at luncheon.

She walked out of the bedroom and was aware that the sound which was now louder came only a little way down the passage from the Master Bedroom in which the Earl had died.

She walked towards it and now distinctly she heard a word spoken several times:

"Nisroch .. Nisroch!"

She thought she must be mistaken for she remembered that Nisroch was the God of hatred.

Then still in a strange incantation she heard two more names:

"Moloch .. Andramalech!"

She knew the first was the dreadful God who devours children, and Andramalech unless she was mistaken, was the God of murder.

"I am imagining this, it cannot be true!" she told herself.

By this time she had reached the door of the old Earl's bedroom and could see it was ajar and the voice came from within.

Quite suddenly she felt frightened.

She had never been afraid in Yarde, which was to her like her own home, but insidiously, like a bitter wind, she now felt fear creep into her body and knew that she was trembling.

Suddenly a low, strange voice cried out clearly:

"Beelzebub, Andramelech, Lucifer – come to me! Master of Darkness, I implore thee, Satan, I am thy slave! Come! Come! Honour me with thy presence!"

Dorina drew in her breath.

Now she recognised the voice and through the crack in the door which she did not dare to touch, she could

80

see, even though the blinds were drawn and the room was in semi-darkness, that her Cousin Jarvis was standing at the end of the huge four-poster bed in which so many generations of Yardes had been born and died.

Now he was saying almost in a confidential tone as if speaking to a person:

"Destroy him, Lucifer! Kill him as you killed William and Charles! Prevent him from returning to England and I swear I will be your slave for ever and will repay you for what you have done for me. Hear me, Lucifer! I will give you any sacrifice you demand – a new born baby or a pure and innocent young virgin – they shall be yours if Oscar dies!"

Jarvis's voice seemed to ring out, then he flung out his arms before he fell onto his knees to say again:

"Satan, I am your slave! Do what I ask of you, and I will never fail you!"

Almost as if she feared Satan might appear to Jarvis in response to his plea, Dorina turned to run along the passage and down the front stairs and out through the front door.

All she wanted to do was to get away; to flee from something so evil, so obscene, that she could not believe that what she had heard was not a figment of her imagination.

Or was she having a nightmare, strange and terrifying, from which she could not wake up?

Only when she reached the quietness of the Vicarage did she feel as if she could breathe normally and was no longer afraid.

She had gone up to her bedroom to throw herself down on her bed and try to tell herself that what she had heard and seen was sheer imagination.

And yet she had known there was a kind of madness

in Jarvis's voice that seemed to linger in her ears, and she felt as if she could still hear him chanting his low incantation of evil names and pleading with Satan.

For a long time she lay on her bed until she heard Nanny calling her and knew that meant that dinner was nearly ready and she must go downstairs and help her.

Because her father had thought there was no necessity for Rosabelle and Peter to be distressed by attending the Funeral, they had been sent to spend the day with a neighbouring farmer and his wife who allowed them to ride the farm ponies and play about in the hayricks.

Dorina had thought his decision wise because Rosabelle had been so miserable and unhappy after her mother's Funeral that she was afraid that another one in the same Church, even though it was for an old man, would reaggravate her misery.

If it did once again she would cry as she had cried for her mother saying that no one else could ever take her place.

When Dorina went downstairs she thought, since she and her father would be alone in the Dining-Room and the children were not returning until later, she should perhaps tell him what she had overheard.

Then she knew she had been so frightened that she would rather try to forget the evil in which Jarvis was partaking.

She had the feeling that if her father knew that her cousin was indulging in Black Magic, for that was what it was, he might feel it his duty to remonstrate with him.

She was quite certain that in that case Jarvis would not only be very rude, but also take some revenge on her.

'I am ashamed of being frightened of him,' she thought.

At the same time there was something menacing and very horrible in the way he had called for the help of Satan.

If he hated her, she feared that, although she believed God would protect her, he might try to put some evil charm upon her.

By the time she reached the kitchen where Nanny was waiting she had made up her mind to say nothing to anybody.

"Forget it! Forget it!" she told her mind, but knew it would be a very difficult thing to do.

Yet now, because she was frightened for Rosabelle, although she tried to convince herself it was ridiculous, she had inadvertently made the new Earl believe that she knew some secret about Jarvis that she would not tell him.

She had the feeling he would be so curious that he would continue to try to extract from her what she had no intention of relating.

"I must have been mistaken at the time because I was upset by the Funeral," she tried to say.

And yet, almost like a banshee echoing round the house, she could hear Jarvis's voice saying:

"Hear me Lucifer! I will give you any sacrifice you demand – a new born baby or a pure and innocent virgin – they shall be yours if Oscar dies!"

All that evening Dorina was very quiet – so much so that even her father noticed it.

The following day she was still wondering whether, if the Earl came to see them, she ought to tell him that Jarvis, far from being friendly and welcoming him, as he thought, was longing for his death so that he could become the 8th Earl of Yardcombe.

Strangely enough, although the children talked about him incessantly, the Earl did not call at the Vicarage the next day.

Peter went up to the stables and came back full of enthusiasm about the new horses that were there and how Hawkins had said he was welcome whenever he wished to ride.

Dorina listened to his excitement a little absent-mindedly, and Rosabelle, who had only gone into the Park with Rover, said enviously:

"You are having all the fun, Peter! I will come up to the stables with you tomorrow!"

"There is no work for girls there!" Peter said. "But I expect Hawkins will let you ride one of the horses."

"I am sure you should ask the Earl first," Dorina intervened.

"I will ask him if you like," Rosabelle replied, "but I know he will say 'yes', and I cannot think, Dorina, why you keep trying to prevent him from being kind to us."

He was certainly trying to be kind, Dorina thought, when at midday, a cart arrived from the Big House containing to her astonishment, food, fruit and six bottles of an excellent claret for her father.

There were chickens, a leg of lamb, and a ham, besides peaches, grapes and greengages from the hot-houses.

"I have no intention of accepting charity!" she said to Nanny. "You can send this back."

"Charity!" Nanny exclaimed. "It's nothing of the sort, Miss Dorina, and you know it!"

"Of course it is charity," Dorina replied, "and at least we should have the pride to realise it."

Nanny put out her hand towards the food as if she would prevent her from taking it from the table and said:

"Read your Bible, Miss Dorina, and see that the people always took offerings to the priests. There's nothing wrong in His Lordship giving the Master gifts of the same sort, and you should be grateful he's kind and generous enough to think of us. Even the old Earl had no idea how hard it was to make ends meet!"

This was certainly true, and Dorina knowing how much her father would enjoy the claret began to weaken as Nanny went on:

"I, for one, am sick to death of seeing the children looking half-starved, and feeling that hungry myself that at times I could eat an ox!"

Dorina laughed because she could not help it. Then she said:

"Very well, Nanny, and as the Earl says he is going to raise Papa's stipend, I suppose we can count this as the first instalment."

Nanny's eyes brightened.

"Increase the Master's stipend?" she repeated. "Well, that's a start in the right direction! Whatever they may say in the village about the trouble there's been this past year, it's obvious His Lordship is trying to put things to rights, and as we are Christians there's nothing we can do but help him!"

Dorina was forced to admit that the Earl's behaviour was certainly a point in his favour.

At the same time she could not completely forgive him for the house-party that had caused so much trouble the moment he arrived.

Even if she conceded that the man who had assaulted Mary Bell was a friend only of Cousin Jarvis, she had seen the way Lady Maureen Wilson had behaved.

She had known then that such behaviour would have shocked her mother and was definitely not that of a Lady of Quality, however much things might have changed in the social circle that surrounded the Prince Regent in London.

"If that is the sort of woman he likes," she said, "then not only should Rosabelle not associate with his friends and Cousin Jarvis, but the less she has to do with the Earl himself the better!"

Once again the thought about her Cousin Jarvis and his sinister behaviour, was with her, and she wondered if she could somehow hint to the Earl that he was dangerous without having to reveal the details of why she thought so.

Then she told herself she was being hysterical.

How could Jarvis hurt the Earl by a lot of mumbo-jumbo of Black Magic? She was quite certain her father would say it was something believed in only by very simple and primitive people, or those who were mentally deranged.

She was well aware that in the countryside there were still old women who were reputed to be witches and could paralyse a man's arm with a curse, turn the butter rancid when a woman was churning it, or worse still, prevent a prize cow from calving.

Had they really any powers? She wondered now as she had wondered once or twice before when girls in the village sought out the witch for a love-potion.

She knew they also sought them out for help in having their revenge on a rival who had stolen their favoured man.

"Evil can only hurt evil people!" her mother had said once when she was told of some curse that had resulted in dire effects according to village gossip.

Mrs. Stanfield was certain that what had happened could be explained as due to quite ordinary circumstances.

"I am sure Cousin Jarvis would not be able to hurt

a man like Papa by Black Magic," Dorina reasoned. "But if the Earl is not a good man, then he might be able to strike him dead, in which case, if I do not warn him, I will never be able to forgive myself."

Yet every instinct in her body shrank from going to the Earl and telling him what she had overheard Cousin Jarvis doing.

"He was making a pact with Lucifer," she could hear herself telling him, then she would see the incredulity in the Earl's eyes, and amusement that she should be so childish and so foolish as to believe such a thing possible.

He would think it incredible that any such thing could happen to him, and to tell it might be to show that she was just a 'country bumpkin' with no sophistication.

He would laugh at any idea of the supernatural, as she was sure Lady Maureen would.

"I cannot tell him . . I cannot!" she decided the next day when she awoke.

Realising it was late because she had overslept, she hurried downstairs to help Nanny with the breakfast for the children, before they went off for their lessons.

"As soon as Miss Soames has finished with me today," Rosabelle announced defiantly, "I am going straight to the stables with Peter!"

Before Dorina could open her lips to protest Rosabelle went on:

"I know why you do not want me to go there! You feel jealous because the Earl has not asked you to ride his horses, nor has he invited you to the Big House, even though you have helped him with the servants!"

"That is not true . . ." Dorina began to say, but before she could finish the sentence Rosabelle had flung her arms round her sister's neck to cry:

"I did not mean it! That was horrid of me, and I am sure the Earl would like you to ride with us on his fine horses which would be as wonderful for you as for Peter and me."

Dorina held her sister close and Rosabelle went on:

"I am sorry, I am sorry! You are so good to us, and sometimes I am a pig to you."

"It is all right, darling," she said, "and I am not angry. Go to the stables with Peter, but just promise me one thing . . ."

"What is that?" Rosabelle asked apprehensively.

"If Cousin Jarvis is there, you will come back at once!"

Rosabelle looked surprised, then quickly said:

"I do not mind promising you that! I dislike Cousin Jarvis! There is something about him that makes me feel 'creepy'!"

"Then just come home if you see him, and you can go another day when he is not there," Dorina said.

The two children hurried off to their lessons, and the Vicar reluctantly remembered that he had a sick woman to visit in the village, and the arrangements for a Christening to make before he could return to his beloved cacti.

He hurried off and Dorina with a little sigh was just beginning to clear away the breakfast things when there came a knock on the front door.

She opened it and found to her surprise there was a handsome young man standing outside, holding his horse by the bridle.

"I think you must be Miss Stanfield," he said. "I am staying at Yarde, and my name is Harry Harringdon. I need your help."

"Of course!" Dorina answered. "Perhaps you would

not mind putting your horse in the stable as there is no one here to do it."

She led him to the stables at the side of the house and having shown him where to put his fine horse in an empty stall, she said:

"Perhaps now you would like to come back to the house?"

She was wondering as she led the way what he could have called to see her about, and thought it rather strange of the Earl to send his friend instead of coming himself.

They went into the Drawing-Room and Harry said:

"I rode to the village to find the Doctor, only to discover that he is away."

"Yes, that is so," Dorina said. "His mother has died and he will not be back for at least three days."

"I heard that from his Housekeeper," Harry said, "and I wondered, Miss Stanfield, if you or your father could recommend any other Doctor in the vicinity."

"Is somebody at the house ill?" Dorina enquired.

Harry nodded.

"It is your cousin, Oscar. His valet fetched me as soon as he had called him this morning, and when I saw him he told me he had been violently sick in the night and he looks now as if he is sinking into a coma!"

"It must be something he ate," Dorina suggested.

"That is what I thought," Harry replied, "but we both ate the same things at dinner, and I am perfectly all right."

"But surely he must have had something else," Dorina insisted. "Did he eat anything strange yesterday? Perhaps some fruit which he picked in the garden, or anything else that you did not take at the same time?"

"I cannot think of anything," Harry answered.

"Or did anybody bring him anything?"

"The only person he saw, apart from the farmers he visited all yesterday," Harry said slowly, "was Jarvis Yarde!"

Dorina stiffened.

"Cousin Jarvis? He is with you?"

"He arrived unexpectedly from London just before luncheon," Harry answered, "and was very pleased with himself because he had taken only two-and-a-half hours to do the journey, while the average, as I expect you know, is nearly three!"

Dorina nodded, then she said quickly:

"Why did Cousin Jarvis come to Yarde so unexpectedly?"

"Just to make himself pleasant to Oscar, I suppose," Harry replied.

There was a hard note in his voice as he spoke which Dorina did not miss.

Then she said:

"You do not think he might have given His Lordship anything to eat that you did not know about?"

Harry did not answer for a moment. Then he said:

"When I saw Oscar this morning he was feeling so weak that it was difficult to ask him too many questions, and I realised he should see a doctor. But now I think about it, he did murmur something about wine, but his voice was so low and he seemed almost unconscious so I did not press him to repeat himself."

Dorina looked at him with frightened eyes, then she said:

"I think I should come to Yarde at once! I will bring some medicine with me, one of Mama's herbal cures. She used to give it to the villagers when they were ill, and they always swore it was better than anything the doctor could prescribe."

"A good idea!" Harry agreed. "While you are getting ready, I will ride back as fast as I can and fetch my Phaeton to bring you to Yarde. I might have come in it anyway, except that I thought it would be quicker to ride."

"If you will do that, it will give me time to pick some fresh herbs that Mrs. Meadows can make up for me in the Still Room. She knows, and so does Burrows, how efficacious Mama's special potions were."

"I had better get back then!" Harry said.

Without saying any more he left the Drawing-Room, walked across the hall and Dorina heard him running towards the stables.

She put her hands up to her forehead as if to force herself to think.

At the same time she was desperately aware that if, as she suspected, Cousin Jarvis had struck down the Earl in some mysterious occult manner that she did not understand, she might be too late.

"Why was I not brave enough to tell him yesterday?" she asked herself.

Then she knew that she might once again be imagining something which had quite a simple explanation.

The Earl might be stricken with one of the fevers which often hit the people in the village and for which the Doctor had no explanation.

Or he might quite simply have eaten something which disagreed with him and had made him sick. That, in a way, was a blessing as it would take away from his body whatever was upsetting him.

"By the time I reach Yarde I expect he will be better," she said reassuringly.

At the same time, once again, she could hear Jarvis making his pact with Lucifer and, despite everything her common sense told her, her hands were trembling.

. . . .

Harry Harringdon was surprisingly quick in fetching the Earl's Phaeton from Yarde and he came back with a groom to hold the horses.

He helped Dorina carry from the house the basket in which there were several small bottles containing the herbal essences for which her mother had been famous.

On top of them lay a number of freshly cut herbs from the garden which had been the pride of Mrs. Stanfield and which, however much time the Vicar might spend on his cacti, he always managed to keep in order.

Sometimes Dorina had thought it was painful for him to spend so much time in a place which brought back to him so vividly his wife.

And yet the plants, herbs and shrubs flourished as if they were tended by 'green fingers'.

She was sure this was because of the love her father gave them, just as her mother had always said that plants tended with love always grew well.

"Do you mean, Mama," Dorina had asked, "that if you tell a plant you love it, it really grows stronger and quicker than if you said you hated it?"

"That is undoubtedly true," Mrs. Stanfield replied, "and I know one must also apply the same thing to people. Love can work miracles, while hatred can do irreparable damage."

Dorina now remembered her mother saying that and thought that it might simply be Jarvis's hatred rather than Satan's magic which had struck down the Earl.

At the same time, as she climbed the beautiful

92

staircase at Yarde she was very apprehensive of what she would find.

She had not been near the Master Bedroom since she had heard Jarvis behaving in such a strange way after the old Earl's Funeral.

Now as Harry opened the door and they went in she almost expected to feel again the fear she had felt then and notice a sinister atmosphere in the large room.

Instead there was only the scent of flowers coming from two big bowls of lilies, and there was also the clean, crisp smell of *Eau de Cologne*.

Then she had eyes only for the Earl.

He was lying in the centre of the great bed, his eyes closed, while his face had an unhealthy pallor that was almost blue and very different from his usual robust appearance.

Because he was so athletic and went riding in all weathers and in Paris had kept up his military parades and duties with his Regiment, his skin was suntanned and he usually looked extremely healthy.

Now, to Dorina's consternation, there was an unnatural paleness about him and deep lines under his eyes.

Harry walked ahead of her to the bed and said quietly:

"Are you awake, Oscar? I have brought your cousin Dorina to see you."

With an effort the Earl opened his eyes, saw Dorina looking at him and said:

"I – I am feeling – extremely ill. Can you – find me a – good Doctor?"

"As Mr. Harringdon has already discovered," Dorina replied, "the Doctor is away, but I have brought you something I am sure will help you feel better. First, however, I want to know what upset you."

93

"I – cannot imagine," the Earl replied, speaking with difficulty, as if his voice which sounded slurred, came from far away, "unless it was – the wine – that Jarvis – brought me."

"What wine?" Dorina asked. "And where is it now?"

There was a pause as if the Earl was finding it hard to think. Then he said:

"Jarvis told me he had – three bottles of a very – special old brandy he – wanted to – give to the – Prince Regent – as a – present."

He drew a breath as if it was hard to speak, then went on:

"He – he however said that – as I was a – connoisseur of brandy – having just come from – France – he wanted me to try – a glass – and although he did not – want to seem – mean – he had not – enough – for Harry – so he – brought it to me – while I was changing – after I had been – riding."

"That would have been at about four o'clock," Harry interposed, "and after that he went straight back to London."

"I – I drank only – half the glass," the Earl went on, "because – I do not like – drinking between meals."

He paused for breath again before he went on:

"I – told Jarvis – however – that I was sure the – Prince would – appreciate it – but as soon as he left the – room I threw the rest away!"

"And that saved your life!" Dorina exclaimed.

"What – what do you – mean?"

"I mean," Dorina replied slowly, "and I am quite sure I am right, that the brandy was poisoned!"

CHAPTER FIVE

For a moment both men stared at Dorina in sheer astonishment, then the Earl closed his eyes and said:

"For God's sake – give me something to make me
able to – listen! I want to – hear what you are – saying
– but – this cursed darkness keeps – creeping up on
me."

"Just stay quiet for a moment, while I get you
something," Dorina said quickly.

She picked up her basket and took it to the table at
the other side of the room saying to Harry in a low
voice:

"I think he has been poisoned by either Belladonna
or Foxglove."

"Why should you think that?"

"He is showing the symptoms of both," Dorina
replied. "Belladonna would account for the bluish
discolouration of his skin which is due to insufficient
oxygen and vomiting, while Foxglove brings on a
drowsiness which often ends in convulsions!"

Harry gave an exclamation.

"Can you do something about it?"

"I am sure I can," Dorina answered. "Fortunately I
made an elixir from my mother's recipes only two days

ago for a child who had been eating some Belladonna berries, which in this part of the world is called 'Deadly Nightshade'."

She took a small bottle out of her basket, shook it well, and poured it into a glass which stood on the table.

Then she took it to the bed and slipping her arm under the Earl's head where he lay with his eyes shut, she held it to his lips saying:

"Drink this, and you will feel better."

She knew another symptom was to have difficulty in swallowing. But after a pause he obeyed her and she managed to tip all the contents of the glass down his throat.

There was another longer pause before he said:

"That was a – strange – taste!"

His voice was already a little stronger and not so slurred as it had been before.

Gently Dorina laid him back against the pillows and asked:

"Are you too tired to hear me? If you would rather sleep, we can talk later."

The Earl opened his eyes and said:

"I would – like to hear you – explain – why you think I – have been – poisoned."

Dorina sat down in a chair near to the bed while Harry leaned against one of the carved pillars listening, she knew, intently.

Slowly and hesitatingly because it embarrassed her, Dorina described to them her horrible experience after the old Earl's Funeral and how she had heard her Cousin Jarvis making a pact with Satan that if Oscar died, he would do anything the Evil One asked of him.

Only when she had finished speaking quietly in her

soft voice did the Earl seem to relax his tension and he said incredulously:

"I can hardly believe – that I am – hearing of such things in England!"

"I was thinking the same thing," Harry said. "If we were in the Far East or in Africa, I would not be surprised, but that your cousin, of all people, even though we are aware he is an outsider, should stoop to murder is something I never anticipated."

"Looking back at when we were children," Dorina said, "I think he always resented that William and Charles had a background that he would have liked to have himself."

"I suppose the temptation of knowing that now there is only one life between him and the Earldom has proved too much for him," Harry remarked.

The Earl had not spoken and Harry, looking at him, said:

"For Heaven's sake, Oscar, you cannot die in such an ignominious fashion after having fought through the war without so much as a scratch!"

"Who says – I am – going to?" the Earl asked in a sleepy voice.

"You are not going to die!" Dorina said firmly. "I know if you do Jarvis will spend all the money in London on riotous living, and the estate will be even worse off than it is at the moment."

Despite the fact that he felt so ill, she saw the Earl's lips twitch and he said with difficulty:

"Still – preaching at me – Dorina?"

Dorina knew he was making an effort, so she merely replied:

"Not at the moment, but I will have a lot to say later!"

She thought the Earl was amused, but she knew he

must rest while she prepared another and stronger dose of what she had just given to him.

She therefore picked up her basket and going to the door beckoned Harry to follow her.

They went outside and she said:

"I am sure you will think I am imagining things, but when I was telling you just now about Cousin Jarvis and how he invoked Satan in that room, I felt the same horror I felt then strike me again."

"I can understand that," Harry said sympathetically, "and it must have been frightening."

Dorina looked up at him to see if he was really sympathetic. Then she said:

"It is still frightening, and I cannot help feeling that somehow he has impregnated the atmosphere with his evil designs and they may hurt the Earl."

"Are you saying that you think the Black Magic, or whatever it is, is still in the room?" Harry asked.

"Either it was put there when he was invoking Satan," Dorina replied, "or else, because he is willing the Earl to die, you can feel the vibrations coming from him, even though he is far away in London."

"You are making me feel creepy," Harry exclaimed.

"I . . I am not being hysterical when I say you have every reason to be," Dorina replied.

"Then what can we do about it?"

"What I would like to do," she answered, "if you do not think it would annoy the Earl too much, is to ask my father to come and remove what evil influence is still lurking here. Then perhaps the Earl will feel strong enough to combat anything more that Jarvis is now concocting."

Harry stared at her.

"Are you going to ask your father to exorcise – I think that is the right word – the Satanic influence

98

you feel? And now I think about it, I can feel it myself!"

"That is what I would like to do," Dorina said, "as long as it will not upset the Earl and perhaps make him angry."

"I will talk to him," Harry said, "while you prepare the herbs."

"That is what I wanted you to say," Dorina replied with a little smile.

She then went to find Mrs. Meadows who, as she expected, was deeply perturbed to learn that the Earl was suffering from some sort of poisoning.

"It must be something he ate," Dorina said as she had no wish to alarm the whole household, or make them suspect what had really happened.

"I'm sure it was nothing the cook prepared," Mrs. Meadows said quickly. "She's been trying to please His Lordship ever since he arrived home."

"I am sure she has," Dorina said. "No, I think that when he was out riding or walking in the woods, he may inadvertently have picked a poisonous berry and put it in his mouth. You will remember how Mama was always warning the village children against doing that."

"That's what it must have been!" Mrs. Meadows agreed. "Men never grow up! I always say they're like children until they are put in their graves."

She helped Dorina to prepare the herbs which she had brought with her, and when they had been strained and there was enough liquid to fill a large glass, Dorina hurried back to the Earl's bedroom with them.

She knew from the expression on Harry's face as she entered the room that they had already talked together and the Earl had agreed to her suggestion.

He was now lying back with his eyes shut. Once

99

again she could see the slightly bluish tinge to his skin and was sure that she had been right in thinking it was Deadly Nightshade or Belladonna which Jarvis had used.

As Dorina knew, it grew profusely on many parts of the estate, and Jarvis would have had plenty of opportunity of finding it in his friends' gardens, or anywhere else in the country where it grew.

She made the Earl swallow the concoction she and Mrs. Meadows had brewed for him, and when she took his pulse she found it was slow and guessed that he might have an irregular heart-beat.

She looked at Harry and said:

"I think it would be a good idea to leave him to sleep, when I am sure my antidote will work against the poison."

Harry nodded, and as they went quietly from the room Dorina was sure the Earl was unconscious and not aware that they were leaving.

Outside she said:

"Shall I fetch Papa?"

"I will take you back to the Vicarage," Harry said, "and we can bring him back in the Phaeton. It will be quicker that way, and I do not want to leave Oscar for long."

"No, of course not," Dorina agreed.

"There should be somebody with him, and as I already anticipated that you would want to fetch your father, I have told his valet to sit with him in case he wants anything."

"I see you are a good Nurse!" Dorina teased, and Harry replied:

"We learnt to look after one another when we were fighting together in the Army. At times one or the other of us was down with fever or on many occasions half-poisoned by the Spanish food which swam in oil."

They reached the Phaeton and he helped her in and once they drove off he said in a low voice so that the groom behind them could not hear:

"Do you think he will be all right?"

Dorina knew he was really asking her if the Earl might die, and she replied confidently:

"I am sure now that Mama's antidote, which has been proved effective dozens and dozens of times, will save him. But I am more afraid, I must admit, of what Jarvis has left behind in that room, and also of what further mischief he is trying to raise from a distance."

"If I had not seen what could happen to Oscar on one glass of wine," Harry said, "I should think that you were imagining all this!"

"That is what I kept trying to tell myself, ever since it happened," Dorina replied, "b.but now I feel very guilty that I did not not tell the Earl at once what Cousin Jarvis was trying to do."

"I doubt if he would have believed you," Harry said frankly, "but now there is no doubt that your cousin is not merely a menace, but an unhinged criminal."

Dorina could only agree with him, and there really seemed to be no point in saying so.

When they reached the Vicarage she jumped down from the Phaeton and appreciated that Harry was tactful enough not to follow her.

Instead he sat outside while she went in search of her father.

She knew that by this time he would be back from the Church where he held a morning Service which usually consisted of a congregation of no more than two or three elderly ladies and himself.

But he considered it his duty to take it, and it was

something he never missed, however many other things he might have to do.

She found him in his Study and saw that he had not yet taken off his cassock.

He smiled as she came into the room and said:

"It is a lovely day, Dorina, and I was just thinking of going into the garden."

"There is something I want you to do first, Papa."

"What is it?" he enquired.

She hesitated before she asked a little tentatively:

"Have you ever conducted the Service of Exorcism?"

She felt as she spoke that it was very unlikely, but to her surprise her father said:

"Often, as it happens, but not for some years."

"You have?"

The Vicar smiled.

"When I was a young man I had a friend who lived in Essex, and in that County it is acknowledged there is more witchcraft than anywhere else in England."

He paused as if he was thinking, and said:

"The Chelmsford witches are famous, and a trial in 1556 ended with the witches being the first in England to be hanged."

"That was a long time ago, Papa," Dorina said quickly, knowing it was a mistake to allow her father to start on a long discourse on things that had happened in the past.

"Well, there were witches, and sorcerers, and spells cast when I was there," the Vicar said, "and as my friend, who was older than I was, had exorcised many different ghosts, curses and evil spirits, I too became, through assisting him, quite an expert at it."

"That is exactly what I wanted to know," Dorina said quickly. "I want you to come now, Papa, and exorcise the evil which Cousin Jarvis had planted in the old Earl's bedroom when I heard him calling up Satan and the gods of hatred and murder."

Her father stared at her.

"What are you talking about, my dearest?"

"I am telling you, Papa," Dorina said in a frightened voice, "that Cousin Jarvis is using Black Magic to try to kill the Earl!"

The Vicar found it so incredible that it took Dorina a little time to explain what she had overheard and to persuade her father that she was not exaggerating what Jarvis was doing.

Then when she explained to him that the Earl had been poisoned, the Vicar said sharply:

"This sort of thing must be stopped at once, and Jarvis arrested for attempting such a crime."

"I doubt if anyone would believe it, Papa, just as you are finding it hard now to believe me," Dorina answered. "First things first! We have to try first to counteract Jarvis's devilish scheming, so I want you to come with me to Yarde to see the Earl, and exorcise the evil which I know is still there in the bedroom and intent on putting an end to his life."

"I will come at once," the Vicar said briefly.

As he spoke he picked up his surplice which he had laid over a chair when he came back from the Church and his Prayer Book which was on the desk, and without saying any more followed Dorina into the hall.

Harry greeted him as the Vicar climbed into the Phaeton beside him, and Dorina was squeezed between her father and the other side.

The Phaeton was really built to carry only two people, but she knew that it would have meant a considerable delay if they had asked for one of the carriages, and Harry had felt, as she did, that time was very important.

It took them only about ten minutes to reach Yarde and when they went upstairs to the Earl's bedroom, the Vicar stopped in the dressing-room first to put on his surplice.

Then as Harry opened the door into the bedroom and went in, they saw that the Earl was asleep.

Because for a moment she was afraid that he might have died in their absence, Dorina hurried to the bed-side and felt his pulse.

To her great relief it was stronger than it had been before she left, and she knew that her mother's antidote for the poison that Jarvis had put in the wine was beginning to work.

She also thought, and she was sure she was not mistaken, that the Earl's skin was no longer tinged with the blue which was so indicative of poisoning by Deadly Nightshade.

She was confident now, unless Jarvis should strike again, that the poison would soon be eliminated from his body.

The Earl's valet, who was devoted to him and had been with him as his Batman in the Army, had moved quietly out of the room when they came in.

As Harry shut the door, Dorina knew her father was ready to start the Service of Exorcism.

She had never heard it before, and she thought the language of the prayers was fine.

She thought too there was something confortingly strong and authoritative in her father's voice when he commanded the evil spirit to go and for the presence of God and His saints to drive it away.

She thought too, perhaps because she was personally so closely involved, that it affected her more than it might have done otherwise.

She was quite certain as her father started the last prayer that the atmosphere in the room had unmistakably changed and, although the blinds were half-drawn, she felt it was filled with sunshine, or rather a light that was not of the earth but came from the Divine.

She knelt down as her father gave the final blessing, making the Sign of the Cross to the North, South, East and West of the room, then once again over the Earl.

As he did so the Earl opened his eyes, but Dorina had the idea that he had been awake for some time and was aware of what was happening.

For a moment there was silence. Then, as if the Vicar felt he had in fact been battling with the Powers of Darkness, he walked from the room to compose himself.

Dorina rose to her feet.

"That was very moving," Harry said quietly, and the Earl said:

"I feel better! Thank you, Dorina!"

Dorina felt as if she came back from a long distance, back to the everyday world where she must be practical and do what was required of her.

She moved to the table on which she had left some of the herbal medicine she had given the Earl before.

There was still enough to fill a wine-glass, and she carried it carefully across the room and lifted it to his lips.

He drank it without comment, and as she took the glass back to the table she knew she must make some more to last him through the night.

The Vicar came back into the room.

Now he had taken off his surplice and in his dark cassock he looked exceedingly handsome and, Dorina knew, thanks to the food that the Earl had sent them, stronger than she had seen him for some time.

"How do you feel, My Lord?" he asked.

"A little better," the Earl replied, "and thank you for coming, and for the Service you have just performed."

"I am confident it will be effective," the Vicar said. "At the same time, after what Dorina had told me, I feel we should do something to prevent Jarvis Yarde from attacking you again."

"I was thinking about that," Harry said. "It is obvious that if he thinks his poison will have killed you, as he intended, he will be waiting in London for news of your death."

"Then he will be disappointed," the Earl replied.

"I was just wondering," Harry went on, "how we can teach him a lesson he will not forget in a hurry."

Everybody in the room looked at him. Then the Earl said slowly:

"It might be a great satisfaction, Harry, to knock him out with one's bare fists, or even to challenge him to a duel, but if he is determined to be rid of me, there will be plenty of other opportunities for him to be more successful than he has been this time."

Dorina gave a cry of horror.

"You mean he will go on trying to kill you?"

"Of course he will!" the Earl answered. "After all, he has everything to gain by my death, apart from the ability to settle his debts, which he is apparently unable to do at the moment."

"How can you bear to know that this could be hanging over your head, day after day, and year after year?" Dorina asked.

"That is exactly what I am feeling myself," the Earl said.

"It is intolerable!" the Vicar exclaimed. "Something will have to be done, and at once! I will speak to Jarvis."

"I doubt if he will listen to you, Papa."

Dorina was remembering as she spoke how she had always thought her cousin had despised her father for being a Parson. Now she understood that he had more reason for doing so than just the fact that they were poor and of no social consequence.

As a Satanist, as Jarvis obviously was, he would hate anyone who was a Man of God, and who believed as her father did, in everything that was good, while he had chosen to worship Satan and all his evil.

"Then what can I do?" the Vicar asked a little helplessly.

"We must do something!" Harry said firmly. "As your daughter has said, Vicar, no man would find it tolerable to live with the Sword of Damocles hanging over his head, knowing that anything he ate might kill him, or that he might be exterminated by a bullet or some contrived accident at any hour of the day or night."

"You are making me feel worse than I do already, Harry!" the Earl said with a slight note of amusement in his voice.

Because he spoke almost naturally, Dorina knew with a leap of her heart that her antidote for the poison was working, and she did not even have to ask the Earl if the feeling of nausea had passed.

He was obviously already much better than he had been when she first saw him.

"Is all this too much for you?" Harry asked quickly. "If you wish, Oscar, we can go downstairs and go on discussing it there."

"As it is my life you are discussing," the Earl replied,

"I would much prefer you all to stay here. I want to hear what is being said and take part in any decisions that are made."

"Then of course we will stay," Dorina said. "At the same time, you must save yourself as much as possible. I know you have been finding it hard to talk, and also to swallow."

"How did you know . . .?" the Earl began, then he went on: "I had no idea you were an expert on herbs as well as having a number of other talents!"

"Everything I know I learnt from my mother," Dorina replied. "All the people in the village came to her when they were ill, and they believed, because what she gave them worked like magic, that she was a White Witch!"

She glanced at her father a little provocatively as she spoke and the Vicar said deprecatingly:

"I am afraid that is true. I myself disapprove of witchcraft in whatever form it takes, but the people around here prefer to believe in magic rather than the fact that nature itself provides a cure for most ills."

"Whatever it may be," the Earl smiled, "I am very grateful for what Dorina has given me! I really thought this morning, when it was difficult to speak and even more difficult to swallow, that I was going to die!"

"That is exactly what your Cousin Jarvis hoped!" Harry said angrily. "If ever I get my hands on that young man, he will not be able to talk or walk for at least a week!"

"When he comes," Dorina said quietly, "he will be more determined than ever that only by becoming the Earl of Yardcombe will he get what he wants in life!"

There was silence as everybody was thinking about Jarvis. Then Dorina said:

"I have an idea!"

"What is it?" Harry asked.

"I am thinking of something you said just now, Mr. Harringdon."

Harry looked puzzled and she went on:

"You said Jarvis will be waiting in London to hear the news of his cousin's death. Supposing, just supposing, we let it be known that he is very ill, very ill indeed? I think Cousin Jarvis might then come posting down to Yarde, ready to take over. Perhaps then we could frighten him somehow by threats, or even by violence, never to do such a thing again?"

Her voice seemed to die away, and there was silence as all three men considered what she had said.

Harry spoke first.

"I believe you are right, Miss Stanfield. The best thing we can do is to make Jarvis realise that we know what he has been doing and if he attempts anything more that might result in Oscar's death, he will be instantly arrested on suspicion of attempted murder and, if it is proved, hanged."

"Do you think he will listen to you?" the Vicar asked.

"I will make him listen!" Harry said angrily. "There is really no alternative, is there?"

The Earl was silent. Then after a moment Dorina asked:

"How will you see that he believes that the Earl is really very ill?"

"I will write him a letter," Harry said decidedly, "in such friendly terms that he will have not the slightest idea that I suspect him in any way."

"What will you say, Mr. Harringdon?" the Vicar enquired.

"I shall tell him that my friend Oscar is at death's door and I feel his relatives should be informed. But since I do not know any of them, I think it important for him to come at once to Yarde, and help me to get in touch with his nearest connections."

"That is clever!" Dorina exclaimed. "For of course, having been abroad with the Earl, you are not likely to know any of his relatives, except Jarvis."

"As you say, except Jarvis," Harry agreed. "He is, in fact, the only Yarde with whom I have been in contact since I arrived in England, and I am sure Jarvis will appreciate that, and will not suspect for a moment that I have any ulterior motive in asking for his company."

"You must be careful," the Vicar said, "not to put yourself in the wrong, Mr. Harringdon, by doing Jarvis Yarde any physical injury, out of which he could make a story to gain sympathy."

"I cannot believe anybody could be sympathetic to a man who is a deliberate murderer!" Harry replied. "For I sincerely believe if Miss Stanfield had not been so knowledgeable that she knew how to treat the poison, we would not be talking here happily at the moment, but arranging a Funeral!"

"Was I really as bad as that?" the Earl asked.

He still spoke slowly, but the slur had not gone completely from his speech and the colour had come back into his face, so that he looked almost like himself again.

At the same time, Dorina knew from past experience that it took time for the poison to be completely eliminated from the system, and she said:

"I think now our patient should sleep, and we should all go downstairs so that he is not disturbed. Now that we have decided what is next to be done, we can go into the details without worrying him."

The Earl was about to expostulate, but she put out her hand and laid it on his.

"Please, be sensible," she pleaded. "Although you may not realise it, you have been through a very traumatic experience, and you must take things very easily. But I do promise you, there is no chance whatever now of your dying."

She thought the Earl's eyes were drooping, but there was a twinkle in them as he replied:

"Very well, Nurse! I will put up with your bullying for the moment but not for long!"

They all went out of the room leaving his valet in charge again, and when they were sitting downstairs in the comfortable Study Harry said:

"I am sure you will think I am being somewhat dramatic, but I feel it would be a great mistake for Oscar to be left alone at any time."

Dorina's eyes widened:

"You mean .. you think that Jarvis might .. kill him?"

"If you want the truth," Harry replied, "I think your cousin is mad! He should be shut away in an asylum, but while he is still at large, we have to anticipate that in his crazy desire to be the Earl of Yardcombe he will stop at nothing."

"You mean . . .?" the Vicar began.

"I mean," Harry interrupted, "that we have to face the fact that he may shoot, stab or bludgeon Oscar to death if his plan to poison him has not succeeded."

He paused for a moment before he added:

"I have been at war too long not to know that an enemy when he is cornered will use any means, however outrageous, to gain his objective and to defend himself."

Remembering the wild, mad note in Jarvis's voice when she had heard him conjuring up Satan, Dorina felt Harry was right.

"What do you . . think then we ought to . . do?" she asked in a frightened voice.

"It would be a mistake for you to be involved in this, Miss Stanfield," Harry replied, "but I have every intention of keeping a watch by Oscar's bed at night, and taking it in turns with his valet for one of us to be always with him."

"Surely I can nurse him too," Dorina objected. "As Papa knows, I have nursed many people in the village when they have been ill and there was nobody else to help them, and I nursed my mother too before she died."

"That is true," the Vicar agreed. "Dorina is a very good nurse, and I think too she must be able to observe the effects of the herbs she is giving the Earl. I remember, looking back, that my wife was often afraid of a relapse in any patient she was treating for as long as the first twenty-four hours after they were on the mend."

"Very well," Harry conceded, "and of course I shall welcome any help Miss Stanfield can give us. But for the sake of her reputation, she should not stay here at night unchaperoned."

"No, of course not," the Vicar agreed.

As he spoke Dorina thought he had not given any thought to her position from a social point of view and was thinking of her as being simply merciful to a sick man.

"I will send my letter to London with a groom," Harry said, "and I am sure that Jarvis will not travel when it is dark. Therefore I and Oscar's valet will be with him tonight and tomorrow. If you come as early tomorrow as you can, Miss Stanfield, with your herbs to treat him, we will keep him quiet, then we will just wait and see what Jarvis does when he thinks Oscar is on the point of death."

"That certainly seems a reasonable plan," the Vicar said.

"I think so too," Dorina agreed.

She rose as she spoke and added:

"I think, Papa, we should now go home, for I want to start brewing some more herbs that Mrs. Meadows can give the Earl during the night, and I will bring a fresh concoction to offer him first thing in the morning."

"The groom will drive you home," Harry said, "and then I will go and talk to Oscar before he falls asleep."

"Let him sleep as much as possible," Dorina begged, "and if you would be kind enough to send a groom to collect the herbs I shall have them ready in about two or three hours time."

"Of course," Harry answered, "and thank you, Miss Stanfield, more than I can possibly express for saving the life of a man who has always been more to me than a brother."

There was a note in his voice which Dorina found very moving, and because she felt shy she did not know how to answer.

Then as she and her father drove away from Yarde, she found herself praying fervently that the Earl would be safe, when and wherever Cousin Jarvis might strike.

CHAPTER SIX

Dorina awoke early, despite the fact that she had found it hard to go to sleep.

She was worrying about the Earl and what diabolical ideas Jarvis would think up next.

She was quite certain he was mad, and that his desire for power and to be the head of the Yarde family had unhinged his mind.

She, however, tried to be practical and went into the garden to pick the herbs that would, she hoped, completely eliminate the last vestiges of the poison with which he had tried to destroy the Earl.

It was indeed fortunate that the Earl had drunk so little of the wine otherwise he would undoubtedly have died.

Now he was alive, but the question was – for how long?

When Dorina had taken the herbs into the house and Nanny was helping her prepare them, she thought that she ought also to give him a tonic that would help him back on his feet again.

The children her mother had treated after they had taken Deadly Nightshade were always limp and listless for over a week, and not well enough to go to School.

She was wondering if she could find anything in the garden, when she remembered that a month ago a friend of her father who was an explorer had sent him a present from China.

It consisted of some cactus roots which delighted the Vicar, but at the same time with them he had sent a strange herb which he said in his letter was very precious in China and was kept only for the Emperor.

He wrote:

". . . it is called 'Ginseng' and is known to have miraculous qualities in giving people long endurance when they travel, and also in rejuvenating those who are growing old.

The Chinese worship this plant and I therefore would get into great trouble if they knew I had sent it out of the country. But I thought it would interest you, and I enclose details of how according to the Chinese Mandarin who gave it to me, it should be prepared."

The Vicar had not been particularly interested in the Ginseng because he was so excited at receiving the cactus roots.

Dorina took it now from the cupboard in his Study where he put it. The roots, of which there were several, were in a Chinese box and with them were the instructions.

Dorina followed them exactly and when the Elixir was ready she thought if it brought the Earl back to good health, it would certainly justify the long journey it had made which had taken nearly a year.

She gave Rosabelle and Peter their breakfast and when they were finishing it she said:

"I have a special treat for you today."

The two children looked up at her expectantly and she went on:

"When you come back after your luncheon, I may perhaps not be here, but Hawkins is sending a groom with two horses for you to ride."

Both Rosabelle and Peter gave a whoop of delight, and Dorina went on:

"You have, however, to promise me that you will not ride in the direction of the Big House, and it would be best too to keep out of the park."

"Why should we do that?" Peter asked.

"Because Cousin Jarvis is coming down from London, and I am sure you do not want to meet him."

"No, of course not," Rosabelle agreed, "but as long as we can go riding, I do not care where we go."

Because she could not bear to contemplate Rosabelle coming anywhere near Jarvis, Dorina had made this arrangement with Harry before she left Yarde yesterday.

Now that she had told him and the Earl how she had overheard Jarvis making his pact with Satan, Harry understood and said:

"I will tell Hawkins what you want, and there is no need to worry Oscar with small things like that until he is better."

Dorina could not help thinking that it was not a small thing to her, but she was glad Harry had agreed and she went home feeling they had planned everything as carefully as possible for the next day.

But how could they know what Jarvis's attitude would be and whether as they actually hoped, he would make another effort to destroy the Earl, in which case, Harry would deal with him.

When she arrived at Yarde, a groom with the Phaeton picking her up at eleven o'clock, it was to find the Earl very much better, and looking more like his former self.

He was, however, still in bed, and as soon as Dorina had unpacked her basket and told him the contents, he became very interested in the Ginseng and said mockingly that he was very honoured to sample a concoction which was kept only for the Emperor.

"I hope you are satisfied that it will not poison me!" he said teasingly.

When Dorina said she was certain he could trust her father's friend he said:

"I cannot really argue with you, Dorina, considering how clever you have been in saving my life with your herbal concoction, even though it does not taste very nice."

Dorina gave a little sigh.

"I am only afraid that Cousin Jarvis will have something worse to give you."

"I cannot believe he would try to poison you again!" Harry interposed. "After all, it was a clever idea to give the brandy to Oscar secretly, so that if he had died there would have been no reason to connect Jarvis in any way with his death."

"I agree," the Earl said. "For Jarvis left several hours before the poison began to work."

"That seems to me rather strange," Dorina said.

"Actually," Harry replied, "while of course there are poisons which work instantly, the Ancient Romans are said to have perfected one which took over two months before it worked, which made it quite impossible by the time the victim died, for anyone to find the culprit."

Dorina shivered.

She did not like to say so, but she could not help

feeling that if Jarvis had used a different poison she might not have recognised it or had the antidote available, as she had in the case of the Deadly Nightshade.

It was bad luck for him that the Earl should have somebody close to him with a knowledge of herbs.

Dorina was sure that in ordinary Society ladies like Lady Maureen would not have had the slightest idea what to do when he was taken ill.

As if once again the Earl could read her thoughts, he said as involuntarily she looked at him:

"I am very grateful to you, Dorina, and I realise that you are thinking that God and His angels protected me."

"I am sure of it," Dorina said, "and this room feels quite different now that Papa has exorcised all the evil from it."

"But the evil is coming back," Harry warned, "and that is why we had better be prepared for anything, Oscar, and not be caught napping."

As he spoke he brought a pistol from his pocket and held it out to the Earl, saying:

"This is loaded. Put it under your bed-clothes where you can get at it quickly."

The Earl took the pistol and said as he did so:

"I do not believe Jarvis will shoot me. If he did he could have no defence against a charge of murder."

"Then .. what will he .. do?" Dorina asked in a frightened voice.

"We shall just have to wait and see," Harry replied, "and by the way, Oscar, I think it would be a good idea to tell your valet to meet him in the hall with the good news of your recovery."

The Earl looked at his friend enquiringly and Harry explained:

"It will make him realise that if he is to dispose of

you, he will have to act fast, and that is exactly what we want."

"I see your point," the Earl replied and Harry left the room.

When he had gone Dorina went to the side of the bed and said to the Earl:

"I have brought you .. something which I would .. like you to .. wear."

From the way she spoke and the colour which had come into her cheeks the Earl realised she felt shy.

He held out his hand and she put into it a small ivory crucifix on a gold chain.

"It belonged to Mama," she said. "You may laugh .. but I feel it will .. protect you."

"I am not laughing," the Earl replied in a deep voice, "I am in fact, deeply touched, Dorina, and grateful that you should take so much trouble over me."

She looked up at him and smiled. After a little pause he added:

"I think – I hope I am right – that now you have forgiven me and are no longer hating me as you did when first I came to Yarde."

The colour in Dorina's cheeks deepened and the Earl said again:

"I am grateful and very deeply in your debt. If I survive, I will try to make up to you for all my precious misdeeds."

"Please, I do not want you to .. feel like .. that," Dorina said quickly. "Already everybody is so much happier at Yarde that it is like the old days."

"That is just what I want," the Earl said firmly.

He saw the look of happiness in Dorina's eyes and thought it was remarkable that anybody so attractive should always be thinking of other people rather than of herself.

Harry came back into the room and said as he shut the door.

"There is a Phaeton coming down the drive and, unless I am much mistaken, it is your Cousin Jarvis coming to gloat over what he hopes is your dead body."

"Then he is going to be disappointed," the Earl said grimly.

"Please, please, do be careful!" Dorina begged.

The Earl sat up firmly against the pillows looking, she thought, magnificent under the red silk canopy with his coat of arms embroidered in the curtain behind him.

He was wearing a silk night-shirt with high frills round the neck, and over it was a light robe of dark blue silk, which made him appear almost as if he was up and dressed.

Harry seated himself by the window which was open to let in the sunshine and Dorina sat on the chair at the end of the bed.

All three of them looked relaxed and at ease, but she knew that both the Earl and Harry were as tense as she was.

She started to pray that things might not be as frightening as she feared.

Suddenly the door was flung open and Jarvis walked in.

He had obviously hurried up the stairs the minute he arrived, for he was not only elaborately and fastidiously dressed with a very high cravat and shining Hessian boots, but he was also still wearing his many-tiered riding-coat as if he had been too impatient to discard it.

As he came into the room he stood for a moment

120

theatrically posed, with an expression of astonishment on his face.

Then he exclaimed:

"My dear Oscar! I posted from London the moment I heard how ill you were, but now, to my delight, I have just heard from your valet that you are better."

"Yes, I am better," the Earl replied, "but it was kind of you to take the trouble to come."

"How could I stay away?" Jarvis asked. "I was appalled at the information which Harry Harringdon's letter contained!"

He then looked at Dorina and said:

"I am surprised to find you here, Dorina! And were you instrumental in nursing our beloved cousin back to good health?"

"That is right," the Earl said. "We have to thank Dorina for making me so much better. In fact I hope to get up tomorrow."

"Splendid! Splendid!" Jarvis exclaimed. "And because I feel this calls for a celebration, I have told your valet to bring us a bottle of champagne."

He smiled at the three people listening to him and said in an ingenuous tone:

"I need some sustenance after my mad rush to get here, and I certainly wish to drink your good health, my dear Oscar!"

"How kind of you!"

The Earl had the greatest difficulty in preventing himself from glancing at Harry or Dorina to express his surprise that Jarvis was playing the same trick again.

A few minutes later Walter came into the room carrying a tray containing four glasses and two bottles of champagne, neither of which had been opened.

"Mr. Jarvis asked for a bottle to celebrate, M'Lord,"

he said as he put the tray down on a table against the wall. "But seein' there's two different sorts of champagne in the cellar, I brought up a bottle of each, to see which Your Lordship prefers."

"Either will suit me," the Earl replied. "Have you any preference, Harry?"

Harry shook his head and Walter opened one of the bottles deftly and filled four glasses.

He gave one to Dorina, walked to the bed to give one to the Earl, the third went to Harry, and lastly he gave a glass to Jarvis, and left the room.

Raising his glass, Jarvis said:

"To Oscar! May you continue to flourish and may you always be as successful in life in the future as you have been in the past!"

"Thank you . . .!" the Earl had begun to say.

At that moment, making them all start in surprise, a huge black bird suddenly appeared flying wildly around the room.

Afterwards Dorina could only think it had come from beneath Jarvis's travelling-coat, having appeared as it were, from nowhere.

It was a large ugly bird, flapping about alarmingly, and she instinctively jumped up from the chair by the bed and moved to the side of the room.

"Shoo it out of the window, Harry!" Jarvis ordered.

The bird, however, swooped over the top of the canopy above the Earl's bed and swung away from the window.

Then while everybody else was watching the bird, which twisted and turned elusively, Dorina saw Jarvis, while still distracting the bird away from the bed, pause for a moment.

The Earl, intent on watching the bird, had put his glass of champagne down on the bedside table.

With a movement so swift that she did not think it possible she saw Jarvis drop something into the Earl's glass.

She knew if she had been watching the bird as had been intended, she would not have noticed it.

But something, some instinct or perception, or perhaps a Power which protected the Earl, made her aware of what Jarvis had done.

She was quite sure that her eyes were not deceiving her, although the movement of his tiered coat, if she had not been already so suspicious of him, would have made her suppose that not his hand had moved against the glass, but the hem of his coat.

He then walked away and was helping Harry drive the bird through the open window.

In a flash Dorina had put her own glass down beside the Earl's and picked up the one she was certain Jarvis had poisoned.

Then she moved away and put that glass down on the tray where Jarvis had put his when he had started to try to drive the bird from the room.

For a moment the two glasses stood side by side, then as Harry and Jarvis had finally frightened the bird into swooping out through the open window, Dorina realised what she had done.

As Jarvis turned round she picked up the glass which he had originally held in his hand.

It all happened so quickly that she hardly had time to think, but only to act, and now as Jarvis walked towards her he said:

"What an extraordinary thing for a bird of that size to fly in through the bedroom window and give us so much trouble! I hope it was not an ill-omen!"

"I hope not, indeed," Harry said pointedly.

Jarvis picked up the glass that remained on the silver tray.

"Now we can return to our drinking," he said, "and I look to you all to respond to my toast, and no heel-taps."

He raised his glass once again.

"To Oscar!" he said and tipped the glass of champagne down his throat.

It was only as he lowered the glass that he realised that all three people were staring at him, each holding a glass in their hands which none of them had drunk.

"What is wrong?" he asked. "Why are you not drinking?"

Even as he spoke the last words were lost as he put his hand up to his mouth, then lowered it against his throat.

There was an ominous silence while still nobody spoke.

"Why are you saying nothing?" he screamed. "Why are you looking at me?"

Dorina was nearest to him and he spat the words at her.

Then as she stepped back in alarm, but at the same time watching apprehensively to see if the poison she suspected he had drunk was working, he suddenly said furiously:

"It is you! It is you, Dorina, who is obstructing me! Well, I promised you as a sacrifice, and that is what you shall be!"

As he spoke he drew from his inner pocket a long, thin dagger, not unlike a stiletto.

Dorina could only stare at him paralysed with horror as he cried:

"Die! Die as a sacrifice to Satan so that I can have – what – I – desire!"

The last words were only a gurgle, half-stifled as he tried to utter them.

Then when he would have struck Dorina through the heart, the Earl, with a superhuman effort, flung himself across the bed.

Jarvis was already only semi-conscious from the effects of the poison which must have been almost instantaneous, and as the Earl struck him from behind he fell forward on top of Dorina, forcing her down on the ground.

The dagger he was holding tore her gown on the shoulder, inflicting a slight scratch on the skin beneath it.

But Dorina's head struck the floor with the whole force of Jarvis's body on top of her.

Then as the Earl and Harry dragged him off her, they were aware that he was already dead and the dagger with which he had tried to kill her clattered to the ground from his lifeless fingers.

For a moment she had been knocked unconscious, but soon she opened her eyes to find herself lying on the bed with the Earl sitting beside her holding a glass of champagne to her lips.

"Try to drink a little," he said.

His arm was behind her shoulders and although she wanted to tell him she had no wish to drink, he pressed the rim of the glass to her lips and forced her to drink a little.

Then as she looked at him with frightened eyes the Earl said quietly:

"It is all right! Jarvis is dead, and once again you have saved my life, Dorina!"

"He had .. put poison into your .. champagne."

"I realised what had happened when I saw you carrying the glass back to the table," the Earl said. "It was very brave and clever of you."

She did not speak, but he knew from the expression in her eyes what she was asking, and he said:

"I have told Harry to take Jarvis's dead body into the room next door, and to send a groom for the doctor. I expect he will find that my Cousin died from a heart-attack after driving down from London at such a speed, then drinking too quickly after so much exertion."

As he spoke, once again the Earl was lifting the glass of champagne to her lips.

"This will make you feel better," he said. "You have had a dreadful shock."

"I thought .. he was .. going to .. kill me," Dorina whispered.

"He was mad!" the Earl said firmly. "But he can no longer menace either you or me, and we can forget him!"

Dorina thought as he spoke how stupid she had been to be frightened for Rosabelle but not for herself.

It had never struck her for one instant in order to fulfil his desires, that she could be the sacrifice Jarvis had promised to Satan.

She supposed it was because she was always thinking of herself as so much older, rather than as the young and innocent virgin that was required in Black Magic.

"Forget it! Forget everything about it!" the Earl said quietly. "You have been magnificent, utterly and completely magnificent! But now I want you to go home. You must not be involved as Harry and I are bound to be when the doctor arrives."

As he spoke Harry came into the room and said:

"You are quite right, Oscar. Dorina must not be mixed up in any of this. I will take her home, and I suggest you rest until the doctor gets here, when we shall have to be very convincing about what happened."

"I shall be!" the Earl replied.

He rose from the bed and Harry helped Dorina to her feet.

"Can you walk?" he asked. "Or would you like me to carry you?"

"No .. of course I can .. walk."

She did in fact, feel rather shaky, but she was determined not to appear weak and helpless in front of the Earl.

She gave him a brave little smile as she said:

"Please .. will you take care of .. yourself .. although now I know that .. nothing else can .. happen."

"I would say it is very unlikely," the Earl replied, "but if you two had not been here to witness what did occur, I would think I was dreaming."

Dorina felt the same thing as she drove back with Harry in the Phaeton to the Vicarage.

She thought it would be difficult even to make her father believe that at Yarde, of all places, there had been poisoned champagne, a huge black bird, and Jarvis, after trying to kill her, dying instantaneously from the poison he had intended for the Earl.

Because she was very quiet Harry said:

"I want you to go upstairs and get straight into bed. I will see your father and tell him what has happened, and ask him to arrange the Funeral. I know your Nanny will understand that you should rest after the shock of seeing your cousin die."

Dorina did not argue, and when they reached the Vicarage she did as Harry had suggested and went upstairs to her bedroom where a little later Nanny joined her.

"I've never heard such goings-on in quiet Little Sodbury!" she said, as she came into the room, "and Mr. Harringdon's right when he says your seeing Mr. Jarvis die has been a nasty shock. Now get into bed, and I'll bring you some hot milk."

"I will be . . all right, Nanny," Dorina managed to say.

But she knew it would be no use arguing with Nanny and Harry was right in knowing she had had a severe shock.

How could it be possible after the quiet, uneventful life she had lived for nineteen years that all these dramatic, terrifying experiences happen one after another?

Then she told herself it was all over: the Earl was safe, Jarvis was dead, and there would be no more Black Magic with threats of human sacrifices again at Yarde.

"No one would believe I was telling the truth," she thought.

Yet she found herself as she fell asleep wondering if the black bird that had appeared so suddenly had been real, or if perhaps Jarvis had hypnotised them all into seeing it.

.   .   .   .

It was not until later in the evening, when Nanny exclaimed over the fact that her gown was torn at the shoulder, that Dorina realised that the scratch on her arm from the dagger with which Jarvis had intended to kill her was inflamed.

She could feel it throbbing and told Nanny she had simply scratched herself.

Although, instantly, Nanny bathed the wound with one of the lotions her mother had made against infections, nevertheless, it was uncomfortable during the night, and the next morning, when Dorina wanted to get up, Nanny insisted she was to stay in bed.

"I'm not going to have any arguments!" she said. "You're not well, and here's where you'll stay until you are better!"

"I cannot leave you to do everything, Nanny," Dorina protested.

To her surprise Nanny laughed.

"You've no need to worry about that, Miss Dorina. I've got two people to help me."

"What do you mean?"

"Well, His Lordship sent Mrs. Meadows over yesterday afternoon when you were asleep to ask how you were. She brought us a great deal more food, and instructions from His Lordship that you were to rest while Mrs. Meadows was to find me some help in the house."

Dorina was listening wide-eyed as Nanny went on:

"She sent me a very nice woman who's had some experience up at the Big House, and she also suggested, and I might have thought of it myself, that we had Mary Bell here for a few months."

"What a good idea!" Dorina exclaimed.

"That's what Mrs. Meadows thought, seeing the girl might be embarrassed just at the moment to go back to Yarde and might also feel nervous."

"Can we really afford so much?" Dorina asked.

"We can afford it, and a good deal more," Nanny replied, "if you can prevent your father from giving every penny away to anybody who touches his heart."

Dorina laughed.

"That is going to be difficult!"

"I knows that," Nanny said, "but I'll persuade your father somehow that 'charity begins at home.' And if His Lordship continues to send us some of his stipend in the form of food, it'll make things a lot easier all round!"

Dorina laughed again.

She thought in fact, it was not a bad idea, but she felt too weak at the moment to think things out and was merely content to do as she was told.

She slept most of the day and although she was curious as to what was happening at Yarde, she knew that if she tried to get up Nanny would stop her.

Rosabelle and Peter were perfectly happy because once again horses had been sent for them after their lessons, and they had ridden over parts of the estate they had seldom visited before and found it a marvellous experience.

"I wish you had been with us, Dorina," Rosabelle said sitting on her sister's bed, "but as the Earl has been so generous, I am sure, as soon as you are up, you will be able to have a horse whenever you want, and we can all go out riding together."

"We must not . . impose on . . him," Dorina tried to say weakly, but Rosabelle replied:

"It says in the Bible: 'It is more blessed to give than to receive'! So it would be wrong of you to try to stop him from giving us horses to ride, and all that delicious food to eat!"

Dorina laughed and Rosabelle kissed her saying:

"Get well soon! Because we are being especially good now you are in bed, I am going now to do my homework, even though I find it terribly boring."

It was her father who brought Dorina news of exactly what was happening.

The Doctor, she learned, had come back from his mother's Funeral and had agreed with the Earl that Jarvis had died of a heart-attack.

His body had already been taken to the Church and the Funeral was to take place early the next morning.

"It will be very quiet since none of the relatives have

130

been informed," the Vicar said. "Later of course, they will be told, but I doubt if any of them will miss Jarvis as he was very unpopular with everybody except his own fast friends in London."

Dorina had nothing to say, and her father went on:

"His Lordship is up, and making a great number of plans for things to be done on the estate. He tells me he is feeling extremely well thanks to some strengthening herb you have given him."

"It was the Ginseng that your friend sent you from China!" Dorina replied.

"I had forgotten about that," the Vicar said. "The cactuses he sent me are flourishing, and are twice the size since the last time you looked at them."

"I will get up tomorrow."

After he had gone Dorina lay thinking that perhaps now the excitement was over and the Earl was safe and busy with his own plans, she would no longer be of any help to him and he could manage perfectly well on his own.

She wondered why it made her feel so disappointed and hurt in a manner that was almost physical.

Then she told herself she was being very childish. Why should he be interested in her when he could manage the estate himself?

He now had the right servants at Yarde, his relations would soon be flocking round him, and the neighbours would be only too ready to be friendly.

It was a depressing thought, though she tried to console herself with the thought that by approaching the Earl in the first place she had managed not only to save his life, but also to make their own lives very much happier and more comfortable than they had been in the past.

How could she have imagined when she was so

despondent and literally lacking the money to buy enough food, that Nanny would now have two women to help her and each meal was more delicious than the last?

Even her father seemed less absent-minded than he had been since her mother's death.

"At least I have achieved something," she told herself.

But she knew that every instinct in her body cried out for more.

She wanted to help the Earl, she wanted him to need her assistance and to ask her advice.

Quite simply, she wanted to be with him.

But knowing that to be an impossibility, Dorina felt the tears come into her eyes and, although it seemed ridiculous, the future seemed bleak and empty.

'It is absurd to ask for more,' she thought unhappily.

And yet she knew she wanted more, very much more, but was afraid to put into words exactly what she did want.

CHAPTER SEVEN

The Earl had woken with a feeling of well-being which was only slightly over-shadowed by the knowledge that he had to attend Jarvis's Funeral at ten o'clock.

Harry was waiting for him downstairs in the breakfast-room and said as the Earl entered:

"Well, at least we have a nice day for it!"

"I refuse to talk about it," the Earl replied. "When I think if the way he has behaved, I consider it a farce, not to say hypocrisy, that he should be buried in Christian ground."

"So do I," Harry agreed. "At the same time I think, Oscar, you have been clever enough to avoid any scandal which would reflect on the family name, and you can thank Dorina for that."

The Earl helped himself from a variety of silver dishes on the side board and sat down at the table.

"I agree with you," he said. "Even now I can hardly believe that a young girl living in a small village should not only have had the bravery to confront someone as evil as my cousin, but also have had the knowledge to prevent his poison killing me as he intended."

Harry poured himself another cup of coffee as he said laconically:

133

"Well, justice has been done, and one could almost say he died by his own hands."

When breakfast was finished they drove in a closed carriage to the Church where the Vicar was waiting for them.

There were no other mourners and the Earl noticed that strangely enough there were no villagers present.

He was therefore certain that, although they had tried to keep secret what had actually occurred, the household at Yarde had become aware that Jarvis had in some way threatened him personally, and the information would have flown through the village like wildfire.

Anyway, there was no one to stand by the graveside as the coffin was lowered into it by the grave-diggers, except himself and Harry, and he felt that only the Vicar prayed for the dead man with any sincerity.

After the Service was over they thanked him but did not talk intimately about what had occurred, although they were well aware that, with the exception of Dorina, he was the only other person who knew the truth about Jarvis's death and the evil powers he had evoked to help him.

The Earl had already made a mental note that the Church was in need of structural repairs, and he thought that it was important that, whenever he was at Yarde, he should attend the Services there on a Sunday.

He was sure, he told himself with a wry smile, it was something which Dorina would expect him to do.

As he drove back with Harry, he was thinking that in some strange way his whole attitude to what was demanded of him in his new position had fundamentally changed.

He had, when he left Paris, been prepared to do a

great deal of reorganising and, as he had said most misguidedly to Richardson, to bring in new ideas and perhaps new people to Yarde.

What he had not anticipated was that he should have to be here what he had been in the War – a leader, a commander, and if possible a hero to his people.

Now in a twisted way, Jarvis had shown him that, although it was something he did not like to think of himself as being, he must be good.

He was so deep in his thoughts that he did not realise that Harry, who was so close to him, understood that he wanted to be silent and did not speak until the horses came to a standstill outside the front door.

Then he said:

"Let us change, Oscar, and I think you are well enough to ride for an hour or so. Nothing strenuous, but I am sure the exercise would do you good."

"That is exactly what I had intended to do," the Earl replied, "and actually I feel extraordinarily well. It must be due to that strange herb that Dorina gave me which came from China."

"I was going to ask you about that," Harry said. "Does it really make any difference?"

"All I can tell you is that I feel better than I ever have in my life! What is more, my brain seems clearer and I can think of a thousand things I want to do."

Harry held up his hands in pretended horror.

"Now you are frightening me!" he said. "I know what you are like when you are planning a new campaign, and expect it to start operating instantaneously!"

The Earl laughed as they walked up the stairs side by side, and he thought he must remember to tell Dorina how excellent he thought her Chinese herb was and ask her to make him some more.

It did not take the Earl long to change and when he came downstairs the horses were waiting.

He and Harry rode over the Park, galloped them on a level piece of ground, and then as it was nearing luncheon-time, returned to the house.

All the time he was riding, the Earl was appreciating, as he had been unable to do before, how beautiful his estate was, and how magnificent the house looked set against the fir woods with the gardens brilliant with colour sloping down to the lake.

No wonder, he told himself, that it was the focal point of the family and that the Yardes, wherever they might be in the world, thought of their ancestral mansion as home.

He and Harry walked together into the Library where he knew there would be drinks, if they wanted them, before luncheon and the morning papers that had arrived.

There had been so much to keep his mind occupied at Yarde, that the Earl thought somewhat guiltily that he was out of touch with what was happening in London both socially and politically.

He had just picked up *The Morning Post* when the door opened and Burrows announced:

"Lady Maureen Wilson, M'Lord, and Sir Roger Chatham."

The Earl looked up in surprise as Lady Maureen came into the Library looking beautiful but over-dressed and over-painted.

She was wearing a gown of emerald green which was matched by her jewels, and ostrich feathers floated defiantly on her high-crowned bonnet.

With a little cry of delight she ran across the room holding out her hands to the Earl and saying:

"How could you neglect me for so long, Oscar darling? It is because I could not live without you that I have come to the country."

The Earl, who had stiffened as she approached him, took one of her hands and raised it perfunctorily to his lips before he said:

"This is certainly a surprise, Maureen. I was not expecting either you or the gentleman accompanying you."

"Roger was kind enough to bring me in his Phaeton," Lady Maureen replied, "and he is convinced that he has broken your record with his new team which is quite magnificent."

As she spoke, Sir Roger Chatham came forward, reached the Earl and held out his hand.

"Nice to be here again, Yardcombe."

The Earl deliberately ignored his hand and said:

"When you were my guest, Sir Roger, at the invitation of my Cousin Jarvis, you abused my hospitality and I can only ask you to leave immediately!"

Sir Roger stared at him and Lady Maureen gave a cry of astonishment.

"What are you saying? What is all this about, Oscar?"

"I am sure Chatham is well aware that his behaviour when he was recently under this roof was not becoming to a gentleman and quite inexcusable."

The Earl's voice was like a whip, and Sir Roger, who had turned very red in the face, muttered:

"I do not know what you are talking about, Yardcombe. In fact, I think you must have taken leave of your senses!"

At the same time his eyes flickered and the Earl was sure he was not mistaken in thinking it was he who had assaulted Mary Bell and upset the whole household and village, thus bringing Dorina to condemn him with an expression in her eyes he never wished to see again.

He knew that it would be a terrible mistake now, from his own point of view, to accept Sir Roger as his guest at luncheon as he and Lady Maureen had obviously intended.

"I think, Chatham," he said firmly, "you would not wish me to go into details, and I suggest you leave immediately. You can either take Lady Maureen with you or collect her after luncheon."

"What are you saying? What are you talking about, Oscar?" Lady Maureen cried. "How can you dare to be so rude to one of my friends!"

She spoke accusingly, but when she saw the expression in the Earl's eyes and the sharpness of his chin, she slipped her arm through his and said beguilingly:

"This is not the welcome I expected, dearest Oscar. If Roger has offended you I know he will apologise, and then we can all enjoy ourselves."

"I can see no reason why I should apologise for anything I may or may not have done!" Sir Roger said aggressively. "I cannot help it if Yardcombe has listened to a lot of lies about me, and my conscience is clear."

"Then you are very fortunate," the Earl answered. "I still insist that I have no intention of entertaining you now, or at any other time!"

"Damn it all!" Sir Roger swore. "This is the outside of enough! I am not going to stand being insulted by you or any other man for some crime he is afraid to name!"

"I am not the least afraid of saying what you did," the Earl retorted. "Perhaps you would like me to call witnesses from the servants' hall to substantiate what I am saying."

The expression on Sir Roger's face proclaimed his guilt without having to be spelt out further.

If he had been doubtful as to what the Earl was referring to, the doubt no longer remained. All he could do was to say angrily:

"I do not intend to stay here and listen to a pack of lies. I thought you were a man of the world, but I see that after all you are only a tinpot soldier with a lot of boring Puritan ideals which are certainly out of keeping in the Social World in which I move."

The Earl did not reply. He merely looked at Sir Roger with a faint twist to his lips and an expression of contempt in his eyes which would have made any man feel vanquished.

For the moment the two men faced each other. Then with a muttered oath Sir Roger turned on his heel and walked to the door.

As he reached it he turned to say:

"I will wait five minutes for you, Maureen. If you do not join me by then I will drive back to London without you."

He left as he finished speaking and Harry tactfully followed him so as to leave Lady Maureen alone with the Earl.

She gave another cry of horror and then throwing back her head to look up at him she said:

"What has happened? What is wrong? Oh, Oscar, I was so looking forward to seeing you! How could you behave in such a cruel and heartless manner?"

"I am sorry, Maureen," the Earl replied, "but I will not have an outsider like Chatham in my house."

"But he has been so kind to me."

"Then I suggest you drive back to London with him."

She reached out her hands to lay them palm down

on the revers of his coat and her lips were very near to his as she said:

"I love you, Oscar. I made Roger bring me here because I wanted to see you – because I wanted to be sure that you still love me as I love you."

The Earl looked at her, but despite the pleading note in her voice, the beseeching look in her blue eyes, and the subtle fragrance of the perfume which accentuated her allurement, he said coldly:

"I think, Maureen, we have both forgotten, and it is very reprehensible, that you have a husband."

Had he thrown a bomb at her, Lady Maureen could not have been more astonished.

She stared at him incredulously and then said:

"Husband? But what has he to do with us?"

"A great deal," the Earl said, "and because I know Wilson and like him, I can only feel ashamed that we should both have betrayed him."

"I think you are crazy!" Lady Maureen exclaimed. "Was Roger right in suggesting you have suddenly developed a Puritan conscience and taken to psalm-singing?"

"Perhaps that is the answer," the Earl replied coolly.

"I do not believe it," she said. "Have you forgotten what we meant to each other first in Paris and then when you returned to London?"

She knew her plea was going unheeded, and in a different tone she said:

"Surely you cannot have become overnight so prim and proper that you now consider a wife must be unswervingly faithful to her husband?"

As she threw back her head she said:

"If that is the truth, then all I can say is that you will be the laughing-stock of everyone in London."

"To be accurate, of a certain section of the Society

140

to which you belong," the Earl said. "My answer is quite simply, let them laugh!"

Lady Maureen gave a scream.

"What you are really saying, Oscar, is that you are tired of me and I no longer attract you."

She spoke as if such an idea was unthinkable, but the Earl replied slowly:

"You are a very attractive woman, Maureen, but I find it unpleasant to think I am stealing from another man what is his, and humiliating not only him, but myself in doing so."

Lady Maureen stamped her foot.

"If you are telling me the truth, then all I can say is you are insane! You, the most ardent and enticing lover I have ever known, are now only fit for Bedlam!"

She stared at him as if she did not really believe what she was saying was true. Then with a quick change of mood she held out her hand and said:

"Oscar dearest, we cannot leave each other like this."

"I think it is the wisest thing to do, Maureen," the Earl said impassively, "and I really believe we have nothing to gain by continuing this argument."

"Then I will go," Lady Maureen replied. "I hate you, Oscar! Do you hear me? I hate you!"

"I am sorry that is how you feel," the Earl said, "but there is nothing I can do about it."

"Nothing?" Lady Maureen cried, and it was half a curse, half a sob.

Realising that the five minutes that Sir Roger had given her must be nearly over, she walked to the door with what was obviously affronted dignity.

It was only when she reached it that she looked back to say, when she saw the Earl had not moved but was standing exactly where she had left him:

"You will be sorry about this, Oscar, very sorry!"

Then she left the room, violently slamming the door behind her.

It was only when he could no longer hear the sound of her feet moving down the passage that the Earl went to stand by the window, drawing in deep breaths of air as if he felt he needed them.

It was some minutes before Harry came back. He took one look at the Earl and walked to the grog-tray to pour out two glasses of champagne.

He placed one in the Earl's hand and said as he did so:

"You were absolutely right, Oscar. Chatham is a nasty piece of work and I am glad to see the last of him."

The Earl took a sip of the champagne before he said:

"I suppose between them they will make up a story which may include a few grains of truth in it and could reflect on the family name."

"I think that is unlikely," Harry said quietly.

"Why?" the Earl asked.

"Because to be thrown out of Yarde would be so ignominious that everyone would know you must have had a good reason for doing so."

"I had not thought of that."

"You forget, my dear fellow," Harry said half jokingly, "how important you are now."

The Earl did not answer. He was merely thinking he had done what he thought was right, and that perhaps it was the influence of the cross that Dorina had given him which he was still wearing around his neck.

· · · · · · ·

Nanny allowed Dorina to get up for luncheon and come downstairs.

The scratch on her arm had healed cleanly and no longer troubled her. But she was feeling a little low-spirited and depressed because, although she had hoped that the Earl would come back with her father after the Funeral, there had been no sign of him.

She had learnt from her father that the Earl and Harry had been the only two mourners, and she could visualise them going back to Yarde together, laughing and carefree because the menace of Jarvis was finished for ever. Now everything in the Earl's future was golden with sunshine.

She knew, without anyone having to tell her, that he had found his inheritance really interesting, and her father had said he intended to explore the gravel-pits which were shown on the old map.

The Vicar had also learnt that the number of wood-cutters was to be trebled, which meant there would be work for a number of young men in the village who had come back from the war to find nothing to do.

"He now no longer needs me," Dorina told herself, and felt the pain of it was like a dagger that Jarvis had intended to drive into her heart.

While she was in bed, Nanny, having the time because she no longer had so much to do in the house, had made her a new, white gown which was something she had not had for years.

It was very simple. The muslin was not expensive, but the best the carrier had on his cart when he called in the village the week before.

The ribbons, which crossed under her breasts from her shoulders and hung down her back, came from an old gown of her mother's and were the green of the woods, making her look very nymph-like.

It also made her think, as she caught a glimpse of herself in the mirror, that she would like to go to the woods to think where, ever since she had been a child, she had taken her joys and sorrows.

She somehow felt that the trees and the spirits of the woods understood her.

When luncheon was over, and since she had help Nanny no longer required her to take away the dishes, Rosabelle and Peter went riding. She had told them they could ride in the Park that day and gallop on the level ground and on the East side of it.

"All I can say is thank goodness Cousin Jarvis is dead," Rosabelle said, "and we can enjoy ourselves as we want to do."

"I think that is something you should not say," Dorina corrected almost automatically.

But she knew as she spoke that she was thanking God with almost every breath she drew that Jarvis could no longer menace the Earl and he was safe.

When the children had ridden away, excited at being on such fine horses, she walked through the garden-gate and into the Park and under the oak trees towards the nearest wood.

In the centre there was a small clearing made many years ago by the wood-cutters, and one of the felled trees was still lying there.

It made a comfortable seat on which she could sit to look at the great house in the distance with the lake below it and the Earl's standard flying against the blue sky.

It was so beautiful that Dorina felt as if the trees all around her were singing a melody which she could not hear with her ears but with her heart.

Then she thought of the Earl, reigning like a King over such beauty, and how wonderful it had been to be with him when he had asked for her help with Burrows and Mrs. Meadows.

144

She had then saved his life with her mother's herbal potions, and to think of it gave her a happiness which was perfect, rapturous and different from any feeling she had ever known in her life before.

She sat for a long time staring at the house and feeling almost as if she was speaking to the Earl and telling him how important it was in her life.

Then astonishingly, because never before had she been interrupted when she was in the woods, she heard the sound of a horse's hooves coming nearer and nearer.

Turning around she saw the man of whom she had been thinking riding his black stallion.

He drew in his horse and for a moment just sat looking at her, silhouetted against the trees in her white gown with green ribbons.

Then he dismounted, tied his horse's bridle to a fallen branch, and came walking towards her through the undergrowth.

He took off his hat as he did so, and she thought how handsome he was and how overwhelmingly masculine. Then she felt herself blush because she had never felt like that about him before.

"Your Nurse told me that this is where I would find you," he said, as he reached her.

"I did not .. expect you this .. afternoon," Dorina said, "or I would have .. stayed at home."

"I am not complaining," the Earl replied, "and I feel, if I am not mistaken, that you are very much at home here in my woods."

He smiled at her and sat down beside her on the tree-trunk. Then he looked, as she had been doing, at the view in front of them and said:

"I am sure you have been thinking about Yarde and all the things I should be doing for it."

"I think you have done quite a lot already."

"There is a great deal more to be done," the Earl replied, "but I think, Dorina, that I should start by thanking you that I am here to do it."

"No, please," Dorina pleaded, "I do not want your thanks. I am only so very .. very glad that you are .. alive."

"I do not think you would have been so glad the first time you came to see me, angry and full of condemnation."

She did not answer and the Earl said as if he were thinking it out:

"I suppose it was a choice between me and Jarvis, and I was the lesser of two evils."

"All that is forgotten," Dorina said quickly. "You made a mistake, but you were big enough to realise it. Now everything has changed."

"Are you quite sure about that?"

"Quite sure," she answered.

"Now I want to know, Dorina," he said, turning sideways so that he could look at her, "what you feel about me."

It was a demand which took her by surprise, and he saw the colour come into her cheeks as her eyes flickered and she looked away from him.

"We have been through," the Earl said quietly, "some very strange and traumatic experiences together. Such as, I should imagine no other two people have ever had! I cannot believe that you still think of me as an outsider who has become the Earl, any more than I think of you just as an ordinary, very pretty girl who is the daughter of the local Vicar."

There was just a hint of amusement in his voice as he spoke, and Dorina asked almost childishly:

"And how do you .. think of .. me?"

"Do you really want to know?" he asked. "But first it is only fair that you should answer my question."

She gave him a very attractive smile before she said:

"That is easy! I think of you as a man who is very suitable to be the Earl of Yardcombe, and will make a great success of it."

"That is possible," the Earl admitted, "but that I am still the Earl of Yardcombe is entirely due to you. I think I should ensure my success by making certain that you help me achieve it."

"That is something I would very much like to do," Dorina answered, "but I was thinking this morning that now you can .. manage very .. well without .. me."

She spoke with a sincerity which told the Earl that it was truly what she believed, and he thought how very different she was from any other woman he had ever known.

Then he said quietly:

"You told me what you think of me as an Earl, but what I am really interested in is what you feel about me as a man."

She looked at him with a faint air of surprise, and he realised she still did not understand what he was trying to say.

He put out his hand, pulled Dorina to her feet, and drew her forward a few steps so they had a better view of the house, the lake and the great trees of the Park lying in front of them.

"We are looking at Yarde," he said, "which you have known all your life, and which means, I know, a great deal to you. But it is all new to me since I have lived twenty-nine years without it. So I have a great desire, Dorina, for you to think of me quite apart from the background of Yarde, and just as I was when I first came here – an ordinary soldier who had made a career for himself in the Army and had no ambitions outside it."

"I think I understand .. what you are asking me," Dorina said, "but I think that everything you strove for and learnt in the Army was only a preparation, planned for you by fate, or as I believe by God, so that when the time came you would not fail those who rely on you and who belong to you because they are your people."

The Earl laughed and it was a very tender sound. Then he said:

"Oh, my darling, only you could give an answer like that, which is so true, but at the same time is not really what I wanted to hear."

At the endearment Dorina's eyes widened in surprise and he said:

"Surely you realise now that what I am trying to say in a roundabout way is that I love you."

"You .. love .. me?"

The words were only a murmur beneath her breath, but her face was suddenly radiant with an almost strange unearthly happiness.

The Earl knew he had never seen anyone look so lovely, with a beauty that was part of the sunshine and of the stars – too exquisite to be human.

"I love you," he said, "but I want you to love me not because I own Yarde, but because I am myself."

As he spoke he put his arms around her and drew her against him.

Before she could say anything his lips were upon hers.

He kissed her very gently, not only because he realised she had never been kissed before, but also because it was impossible for him to think of her with anything but reverence. There was something holy about her that he had never encountered previously.

Then as he felt the softness and innocence of her lips, his own became more insistent, more demanding, and as she trembled against him he felt that he was trembling too.

Everything about Dorina was so different from the passionate, promiscuous women he had known in the past, that he was half afraid he was dreaming and she would fly out of his arms to vanish like an illusion that was part of his imagination.

Then as he raised his head, Dorina said to him in a rapt little voice that was no louder than the whisper of the trees:

"I .. love .. you! I .. love .. you, but I did not realise that what I felt .. was love."

"What do you feel now?" the Earl asked.

"That you are .. so .. wonderful, so .. god-like, it cannot be true that you .. love me."

"I would take a long time to tell you how much," he replied, "but thanks to you we have all our lives in front of us, and I shall love, adore and worship you, knowing that our happiness will make everyone that we know happy."

Dorina made a little sound and hid her face against his shoulder.

"You are not crying, my darling?" he asked. "Have I said something to make you cry?"

"It is .. only that I am so .. happy," Dorina said in a tremulous voice. "I thought today that now you were safe and had .. everything you wanted, you would no longer want .. me."

"What I want above all else, is you," the Earl said. "I cannot, and this is the truth, my precious, live without you."

"How can you .. possibly feel like .. that?"

"It is not only possible, but something I shall find increasingly true hour by hour, day by day, every year of my life."

He gave a sigh as he held her still closer.

"You are what I have always been looking for but was quite certain I would never find since you did not even exist!"

He put his fingers under her chin and turned her face up to his.

"How can you be so beautiful and at the same time so sweet, unspoilt and unselfish? And how can I have been lucky enough to find you?"

"I am afraid that since I have always lived here in Little Sodbury," Dorina said, "when you know me better you will perhaps be .. bored and want to return to the .. exciting ladies you .. knew in London."

He knew as she spoke that she was thinking of Lady Maureen, and he said:

"I have something to tell you, my precious, although it is not immediately important. However I expect that by the time you get home the news of what has happened will have reached the Vicarage."

Dorina's eyes widened.

"What has happened?" she asked anxiously.

"Just before luncheon," the Earl said, "Sir Roger Chatham arrived and I threw him out of the house."

She did not speak and he said:

"That is what I thought you would want me to do."

Dorina gave a cry.

"But of course I would want you to do so! Now everyone will know you did not approve of his behaviour with Mary Bell, and it will make them admire you more than they do already .. and also .. trust you."

"I knew you would understand," the Earl said. "I must tell you also that Lady Maureen came with him, and I sent them back to London together."

Dorina's eyes flickered and he knew what she was feeling. He said very quietly:

"That is all over and finished. Again Dorina, I made a mistake and admit it was wrong to get myself involved with a married woman."

"Was .. she very .. upset?"

"She was incredulous and very angry! But I want you to understand, and I do not wish to discuss it further, that entirely owing to you I now realise what is right and honourable and good in life. That is what we together will strive for in the future, for ourselves and for our people."

"Can you really be saying this?" Dorina asked.

"I am saying it and truly believing it," the Earl said. "I am wearing around my neck, darling, your mother's cross, and I have the feeling that when we are married and are together by day and by night it will help me make the right decisions in all the problems which arise."

Now the tears filled Dorina's eyes and fell down her cheeks.

"How can .. you say .. things like .. that?" she said in a broken voice. "How can .. you .. be so .. magnificent and at the same time .. everything a man .. should be, especially one .. who is the .. Earl of Yardcombe."

The Earl smiled.

"I thought we should get back to Yarde!" he said. "At the same time, my darling, this is all due to you and perhaps to Jarvis too, although it seems a strange thing to say!"

Then before she could speak he pulled her close to him again and said:

"How soon will you marry me? I want you with me at Yarde, and there is so much to do here on the Estate that I cannot allow you the time for a long honeymoon even though it will be a very wonderful one."

Dorina gave a little laugh and it was like the song of the birds at dawn waking up with the sunrise.

"You are going too fast! I have not yet said I will marry . . you."

"Would you dare to refuse me?"

"I am just a little . . frightened that I am not the right person . . for you."

She looked away from him for a moment over the view and said:

"I never in my wildest dreams thought I should live at Yarde and be the wife of the man who owned it."

"And who else, except you," the Earl asked, "would understand how important it is or how much it means to so many people?"

"That is what I mean," Dorina said, "and why I am frightened of being your wife in case I . . fail you."

"You will never do that."

"How can you be . . sure?"

"Because you have the perception and instinct for doing what is right the moment it is necessary, without hesitation and perhaps without conscious thought."

"If that is what I do," Dorina said, "it is because God helps me."

"I know," the Earl said seriously, "and that is why I need your help, Dorina. In fact, I cannot manage without it!"

He smiled and she felt as he did so, no man could look more attractive. Then he said in a beguiling voice which made her heart turn over in her breast:

"Now I ask you again. How soon, my precious, protector and guide, will you marry me?"

"Whenever .. you want me."

"That is what I wanted you to say."

Then he was kissing her, kissing her wildly, passionately and demandingly, until their hearts were beating frantically and he felt her whole body quivering against him.

"We will be married immediately," he said, "and unless you particularly want something different, my darling, very quietly."

"I know what you are saying," Dorina answered, "and it is what I want too. I should feel frightened if there were crowds of your fashionable friends there, criticizing me and perhaps hating me for taking you .. away from .. them."

The Earl did not interrupt and Dorina went on:

"But I think you will understand that everyone in the village and on the Estate should come to our wedding, because just as they belong to you .. you belong to .. them."

"As you do," the Earl said.

"They would be hurt and distressed if they could not be with us when we are married and I think . . ."

Dorina paused and looked at him a little shyly under her eyelashes as she said:

"I think they will expect to drink your health in ale and perhaps have fireworks on the lawn afterwards.'

The Earl laughed.

"I understand exactly what you are saying, my darling. They will all be invited and will have all the ale they can drink, all the food they can consume, and, of course, fireworks so that they will not feel defrauded of a very important occasion."

"I knew you would understand."

"And there is something else I understand," the Earl

said, "which you have forgotten as no other woman would have done."

"What is . . that?" Dorina asked anxiously.

"Your trousseau, my precious! But I daresay we can manage to send to London for enough gowns to make you happy, and I will organise that as well as the fireworks."

Dorina put her hands against his shoulder.

"You think of everything," she said, "and I honestly had . . forgotten. I would very much look the Goose Girl at the feast dressed as I am . . now!"

"You look lovely in everything I have ever seen you wearing," the Earl said, "but just as you know what is expected of me as the Earl of Yardcombe, I know what will be expected of you as the Countess, and you shall have, my darling, the most expensive and beautiful trousseau any bride could ever want."

Dorina drew in her breath and then she said:

"All I want is that you should think I look pretty."

The Earl once again turned her face up to his.

"Whatever you do or do not wear is immaterial. What I shall be looking at, my precious one, are your eyes which mirror your soul, a soul which is so beautiful and so perfect that I want to go down on my knees and thank God for it."

He spoke with a seriousness which made every word that he said seem to vibrate in the quietness around them.

Then, as if her loveliness and the radiance in her eyes made it impossible for the Earl to go on talking, he was kissing her again.

Kissing her with long, slow passionate kisses which drew her heart from her body and made it his.

Then she knew that they were already one in their minds and that no ceremony, however sacred, could make them closer in their hearts than they already were at this moment.

She was his and he was hers, and the Divine Power which had carried them through so many strange and terrifying experiences had brought them finally together with the love and magic which was to be theirs for all Eternity.

Coming next in your collection of
The Romantic Novels of
BARBARA CARTLAND

LOVE LEAVES AT MIDNIGHT

As she turned her face round to his, he said in
a voice she hardly recognised:

"It is agony to leave you, you know that,
and my whole body burns for you. I think
too, my precious, that there is a little fire
burning in you that has not been there
before."

Xenia looked into his eyes and he saw the
answer without her speaking.

He kissed her once again, then walked from
the room as if he was a soldier going on
parade.

Xenia gave a sigh of sheer joy . . .

This was love, as it was meant to be; love
which not only united a man and a woman as
human beings, but which had taken them up
to the Heavens so that their very passion for
each other was sanctified and made holy.

"He is so wonderful!" she thought.

Have you placed your regular order for
**THE ROMANTIC NOVELS OF
BARBARA CARTLAND**
with your newsagent yet?
Don't forget that if you place a regular order
you will receive a beautiful **free** copy of
Barbara Cartland's book of poetry
LINES ON LIFE AND LOVE
(you may cancel this regular order by
giving your newsagent two weeks' notice,
so you are not entering into any long-
term commitment)

If you have any difficulties in getting hold
of a copy, please write to:
Barbara Cartland's Romantic Novels,
Eaglemoss Publications Ltd.
7 Cromwell Road,
London SW7 2HR
or telephone 01 581 1371